O9-BSU-267

THE LISBON SYNDROME

THE LISBON SYNDROME

Translated by Paul Filev

EDUARDO SÁNCHEZ RUGELES

Turtle Point Press
Brooklyn, New York

First published in Spanish as *El síndrome de Lisboa* in 2020.

Turtle Point Press
208 Java Street, Fifth Floor, Brooklyn, NY 11222
info@turtlepointpress.com

Library of Congress Cataloging-in-Publication Data
Names: Sánchez Rugeles, Eduardo J., 1977- author. | Filev, Paul, translator.
Title: The Lisbon syndrome / Eduardo Sánchez Rugeles ; translated by Paul Filev.
Other titles: Síndrome de Lisboa. English
Description: First edition. | Brooklyn, NY : Turtle Point Press, [2022]
Identifiers: LCCN 2021040767 (print) | LCCN 2021040768 (ebook)
ISBN 9781933527543 (trade paperback) | ISBN 9781933527550 (epub)
Subjects: LCGFT: Novels.
Classification: LCC PQ8550.429.A5555 S5613 2022 (print) | LCC PQ8550.429.A5555 (ebook) | DDC 863/.7--dc23
LC record available at https://lccn.loc.gov/2021040767
LC ebook record available at https://lccn.loc.gov/2021040768

Printed in the United States of America

To the fallen.

Everything hurts me on this day
in which the dead lay at the door
of the living
corrosive melancholy.

–Eugénio de Andrade

O *Portugal, today you are the fog.*

–Fernando Pessoa

I swear on my life
that I have come to beseech you for
the Apocalypse of Hope.

–Carlos de Oliveira

Contents

I

Overture: Dies irae

A YEAR AFTER THE disappearance of Lisbon, the world was still in the same place. The doomsayers had to resign themselves to the relentless passing of the days and hours, as if nothing had happened, as if the loss of more than five hundred thousand souls had been a fleeting and insignificant event. The Last Judgment, heralded by fanatical prophets, was suspended until further notice. Life continued on its errant course, despite the fact that, as experts claimed, the planet's axis had suffered a serious and imperceptible shift. The tides and the winds became erratic and unpredictable. A mass of fog blanketed the sky, spreading over the Caribbean. The sun, however, continued its quiet journey behind the fog. And after many anxiety-filled months, the peoples of the earth learned to live with the memory of the tragedy.

Though human life went on, there is a "before" and an "after" Lisbon. Ever since the mouth of the Tagus was struck, people's day-to-day lives began to feel empty and meaningless. The calamity that destroyed Portugal was a tear in the fabric of the world, a turning point in a macabre and absurd story line, reliable evidence of our helplessness in the face of God's unpredictable design of either chance or nothingness.

• • •

A year after the disappearance of Lisbon, I'm still in the same place. It's cold. Flies swarm around the dirty napkins strewn on the floor. The TV mounted in the corner of the bar flashes images of a charity concert. I had no idea it was one year since the disaster. Giménez was the one who remembered: "They really fooled us with that end of the world stuff! And yet here we still are. A real shame!" He was cleaning beer filters. He seemed to be talking to himself, annoyed at his own good luck. Visions invaded my mind, as if the disaster were a recent event. Tatiana's tears dominated my memory. The end of Lisbon coincided with our breakup.

I focus on watching the concert to distract my thoughts. I recognize The Edge from U2. He looks aged and is dressed in black mourning clothes. "Live in Berlin. *Lisbon Forever*" reads the news ticker at the bottom of the screen, displayed below a tide of people commemorating the anniversary of the catastrophe. The sound is off. Giménez watches TV daily but never listens to it. I sit up in my chair and lean my elbows on the bar. The plastic-wrapped remote control lies next to a stack of glasses. I turn up the volume. The sad song filters through the dusty speakers. The screen is covered in an oily film that has turned Bono's face a sickly yellow, as if he has hepatitis. I look around, focusing my grief on the photographs hanging on the wall and the brass medals hanging in a small trophy cabinet. The noisy midday crowds have died away, deterred by the shortages and high prices. Giménez cleans the old worn-out siphon filters, waiting for the patrons who won't come back, but whose comings and goings, joys and sorrows make up the private history of Colinas de Bello Monte. I close my eyes. I remember Tati's hug. The first rumors of what had happened on the other side of the world brought us closer again. Fear of the unknown revealed the depth of our connection. And for a few hours, while we didn't know what was going on, when all we knew was that in some distant place the unthinkable had happened, we got one last shot at being together, before our love entered its final throes.

The information was vague. As usual, the media opted for censorship. Internet and phone services went down. The loss of social media led to the despair of those who'd replaced the disappointments of reality with an alternative virtual life. All we knew was that an earthquake or something similar had devastated a part of Europe, and that an aftershock could happen at any moment. Concern for the fate of loved ones sent new parishioners flocking to the churches, because many of the children and siblings of our friends, of our neighbors, of our housing estate, of our city, of our country had long since left the continent in search of lost peace. And in the streets, the bakeries, and the supermarket lines, the idea began to circulate that the end of the world had begun. The Iberian Peninsula had disappeared, some of the more vocal said. On the third day, when worry gave way to anxiety and uncertainty, and the fanatics threatened to burn down the embassies, the military high command reported on radio and television what for the rest of the world was a confirmed and reliable fact. I had a hard time believing it. Tati cried on my shoulder, repeating in a low voice: "Oh God, oh God!"

The city of Lisbon had suffered untold damage. "Venezuela offers its support and solidarity to the Portuguese people and its deepest condolences to the Portuguese community in our country," stammered a fresh-faced minister.

A year later, and I'm sitting here, incredulous and apathetic, watching the concert at Giménez's bar. With nothing to do, with nothing to lose, with my emotions stirred up by Moreira's revelations, Tatiana's abandonment, and the indelible scars from our last few fights . . . from our many fights. In Berlin, Lady Gaga sings a piano ballad. Stunned and moved, the crowd watches her in silence. Explosions sound in the distance. The battle on the Francisco Fajardo Highway rages on. Plumes of dust waft in. Every now and then, a shot or an impassioned and desperate harangue for freedom can be heard. The fighting is part of the landscape, but there is no hope or ambition. All that remains is the unending weariness of our nullified lives and the ebbing flames of the resistance, doomed to be extinguished.

Allegretto

THE FISSURE WENT UNNOTICED. It was a day like any other when the cataclysm occurred. Months later, the superstitious neighbors would find "hidden signs" while recalling the fatal hours. But they were just lurid and baseless fabrications. While Portugal burned, we slept. My phone alarm didn't go off. I was awoken by the sound of the shower. The kitchen was a mess, with dirty plates from lonely dinners piled high in the sink. I heated some water to make tea. I needed a coffee, but we couldn't get any. Good but exorbitantly priced coffee was only available at the Cine Cittá. Ascanio occasionally worked miracles and would get some in, but it was a revolting, bitter instant coffee. The bread was stale and had blue spots on the sides. The jam hid the mold. Tatiana came out of the bathroom. She grabbed her clothes from the living room chair. We didn't look at each other. We didn't speak. The explosion was coming, but we preferred to contain it, to avoid the wreck. She removed the towel from her hair. I liked her long brown wet hair, every day ever more out of reach. She finished dressing. Anxiously, she checked the messages on her phone. She couldn't connect to the network. Her face twisted into a grimace of annoyance. I went into the bathroom with the memories of better times, when infatuation had shaped our daily life. Dirty clothes on the floor. Strands of hair in the drain. There was no hot water; she had used it all on purpose. The tiny shower, with a torn curtain, conjured up the ghosts of a couple in heat. She took her bag and left. She didn't say goodbye or kiss me on the head, as she had in the good years. She didn't tell me about her uneasy dreams or her afternoon work appointments. She said only one phrase, as an aside. It was technical difficulties that made her break our vow of silence: "There's no internet." Then she vanished out the door. While I wallowed in my own self-pity, millions of people were burning to death under a fiery rock, but I didn't know this at the time.

The sky was a gray mass, heavy and motionless. The summit of Mount Ávila was shrouded in thick mist. On the bus, people struggled with their useless cell phones. Passengers, who were once cautious and mindful of bandits, abandoned all caution due to the breakdown in service. Technological withdrawal symptoms forced them to take out their devices and restart them, change the batteries, blow on the charging port, or bang them against the seat. Virtual life suddenly disappeared, taking with it the feeling of security and enjoyment. Mistrust spread among the travelers. People didn't know how to make small talk. Everyday life was subject to censorship. The window was the ideal excuse not to have to look at each other, but the urban landscape was also intolerable. Families stood congregated around utility poles and broken traffic lights, the trash bags leaning against them hiding the promise of a few tasty morsels. The street smelled of rotten vegetables. But the putrid smell hardly bothered us. We had long become used to decaying things. The stench, like the worm-infested gutters, was normal. It was just the way the world smelled.

That morning, I had to teach at Santo Tomás de Villanueva School. I gave the students a pair-work activity and then graded tests. The topic of everyone's conversation was the collapse of the internet. The kids were lost, distracted and anxious, with their eyes fixed on the screens, waiting for their reconnection with "real life." I ran into Julia in the staffroom. Her face was red, swollen, and streaked with mucus and tears. She was the first person to tell me that something serious had happened. What she recounted sounded like a plot straight out of a sitcom: a trusted neighbor, the wife of an army guy, had received the news, and he told her on condition that she couldn't tell anyone about what had happened. It sounded like an exaggeration to me. I just dismissed it. Rumors and gossip had no basis in our doomed city where nothing ever happened but where disaster was always imminent. After midday, the idea of Armageddon began to gain strength. State TV maintained its regular programming of tedious political talk shows and old cartoons. For a long time, the sitcom *El Chavo del Ocho* had become the official mouthpiece of our silent rebellion. The general feeling was one of fear and dread. Uncertainty plagued our thoughts. Without being alarmed, I imagined it was an al-Qaeda attack, a devastating earthquake, or, in the worst case, a huge iceberg that had broken off from a glacier in northern Greenland and that would flood the rest of the planet for fifty million years. The airspace had been shut down, said those arriving from La Guaira. Flights to Europe had been canceled. Rumors of a coup d'état were whispered around the tables in the bars of Colinas de Bello Monte, but the theory of the Great Flood seemed to have more credibility than our insular concerns.

In the afternoon, I had classes at Promesas Patrias, the old high school perched on the mountain, where I'd been working for the past twenty years. The majority of students were absent. Few had come, just the usual ones: Mimi, Andrea, Jean Carlo (or "Jeanco" for short). We did nothing (we never did anything): they just rehearsed the play, reading the entire piece without paying attention to the signs announcing the end of the world, as if the possible extinction of the human race had nothing to do with them. That night at Giménez's bar, I got embroiled in a discussion with Ascanio and Wong, listening to their absurd theories. Leonidas stuck to his theory of an induced earthquake while Antonio speculated on a devastating, deadly alien invasion. Antonio Wong had moved to Venezuela from China as a child. He was the owner of La Buhardilla, a popular Spanish tavern converted into a Chinese restaurant. Ascanio's stationery store was on Avenida Miguel Ángel. Leonidas was the friendliest *bachaquero,* or black market dealer, in all of Colinas de Bello Monte. There was no greed on his part. His reselling of goods was driven by necessity rather than profit. He wore a wine-colored sweater, which he never seemed to change. The more upmarket peddlers of Cervantes Street, his bitter opponents, played off against each other daily, engaged in useless diatribes. I didn't mind sitting at the bar and listening to Ascanio and Wong talk. I didn't want to go back to the apartment. Tati's coldness, the possibility that she was hiding something from me, was as painful as it was certain. Eventually, we would have to talk about our failed relationship. A part of me wanted to avoid that moment. I didn't have the strength to hear her tell me she'd fallen in love with someone else. The cataclysm was our last chance to save our relationship.

When I got out of bed, when I was able to take two steps and get over the shock of what had happened to Portugal, it was inevitable that I would think of Moreira. Tatiana's hair was splayed across her tear-soaked pillow. The tragedy had dissolved our inhibitions. We found it impossible to sleep knowing that the world, our fragile little world, could be blown to pieces at any minute. We felt fear more than pity. The real possibility that a fireball would cross through the sky and crash into Mount Ávila kept us on edge, stretching our nerves to a breaking point, and making a mockery of our agnosticism. The complete lack of information exacerbated our anxiety, because, with the loss of social media, we had no trusted sources, no alternative versions, no parallel accounts, and no reassuring words with which to deceive ourselves, to tell ourselves that we had been chosen, or that, by God's command, we were tasked with building an ark. After the government's official statement, an all-pervasive silence imposed itself. As in the agoras of ancient times, neighbors gathered in the streets, chatting and adding their own fears and uncertainties to the incomplete account of the disaster. And from the windows you could hear the heartbreaking cries of those who had relatives in Europe. "We're going to die, Fernando, we're going to die!" Tati repeated with wide, tear-stricken eyes. A selfish part of me was grateful for this misfortune, because Tatiana hadn't hugged me like this in a long time. She fell asleep in my arms, the way she used to do when we started dating and moved to Avenida Casiquiare. I sang one of those awful songs she liked to unwind to softly in her ear.

The dawn sky was a pale ashen gray. Somewhere behind the immobile clouds you could sense the presence of the sun, but it would be a long time before we saw it again. I took a walk. The streets of Colinas de Bello Monte were shrouded in thick fog, overtaken by unusually cold weather, as if the waves of the Guaire River were bringing in icy currents of air. The city was deserted. "Closed for mourning," read a sign on the façade of the La Espiga bakery. The trash bags leaning against the broken utility poles had not been split open yet. The tragedy had taken away our appetite. I walked to Santo Tomás de Villanueva. I took the mountain route instead of the usual way through Las Mercedes. There were no classes that day, but a small group of teachers and students met in the schoolyard, with nothing to say, withdrawn, absent, unable to come to terms with the idea of our imminent extinction. As we stood around trying to make conversation, a tsunami of rumors was racing across the Atlantic toward La Guaira. If a student spoke loudly, if they kicked a ball enthusiastically or dared to laugh, they were met with severe looks. The image of the Abreu family popped into my head. It had been more than a year since they moved back to Portugal. I had taught all three brothers. I knew the mom. They were fleeing the absurdity, the shortages, the depravity. They had their citizenship reinstated and they settled in the Chiado neighborhood. I pictured them sitting in class, shooting their hands up to answer questions, running around the schoolyard, and then, one by one, being burned alive or crushed to death. My introspection brought Moreira's name to mind again.

The Centro Polo apartment complex had become an exclusive place. The Cine Cittá, a restaurant-cum-bodega on the ground floor, was a favorite haunt of the well-heeled. There were no government-regulated prices or bare shelves in the aisles. The range of gourmet products (meats, cheeses, wines, craft beers) that lined the bodega shelves warranted the high prices. The luxuries on offer, priced in US dollars, raised suspicions among the neighbors, because no other stores in the area had available the goods that were for sale in the most popular restaurant in Colinas de Bello Monte. The place was frequented by local dignitaries (unknown but famous), nouveau-riche military officers, and politicians on the rise. The old neighborhood never got used to the loud and flashy restaurant in one of the city's most nondescript shopping malls. But its arrival transformed the atmosphere, creating a bubble of abundance in the middle of nowhere. Not being isolated came at a price though. For many years, Colinas de Bello Monte was protected by the imposing Mount Ávila, the swollen Guaire River, and the boundaries of the Las Mercedes and Los Chaguaramos neighborhoods. But when they opened the Metro station and built the overpass connecting the main avenue with the highway, paradise was lost. They opened the door to crime, to the *colectivos* (pro-government paramilitary groups), the *motorizados* (pro-government armed motorcycle gangs), the National Guard's roadblocks and security checks, and the high-end venue for the revolutionary aristocracy, the Cine Cittá restaurant.

• • •

Moreira's home was austere. I had never visited him before. I knew he lived in the Centro Polo but I didn't know the floor or the apartment number. Pantera or Panther, as he was called, performed various duties at the apartment complex.

Not only was he the caretaker of one of the towers, he was also a security guard and a *bachaquero*. When I asked him for the old Portuguese man's apartment number, he reluctantly gave it to me. The living room smelled musty and damp. The cluttered bookshelves kept me distracted while I waited. Old, threadbare editions of Presença or Dom Quixote books were scattered everywhere. My visit did not surprise him. I had the impression he'd been waiting for me, that he'd reserved a place for me at the rectangular table near the window. He greeted me with his usual reverence, with his polite and courteous manner that Wong and Ascanio made fun of. He offered me a glass of water, pulled out a chair, and invited me to sit down. It was no secret to anyone that Moreira was caring for his ailing wife, Señora Agustina. On weekends, it was common to see them out walking, with Pantera's assistance, though nowadays they went out less and less because of the crime and the curfews. Moreira and Agustina were an old childless couple, who arrived from Portugal while democracy was suspended there. When I first met my patron, his wife had already begun her slide toward an irreversible vegetative state. We had only spoken together at La Sibila. Occasionally, we would bump into each other in the aisles of the Central Madeirense supermarket or near Giménez's bar, but I never took the initiative to visit him. The disaster in Lisbon gave me an excuse. I wanted to know how he was, how he felt, to ask him if he had family in Portugal or if I could do anything for him. The uncertainties thrown up by the catastrophe made me realize I knew nothing about Moreira. While this peculiar old man had given me his complete trust, I had never shown interest in his life. We talked about Lisbon without going into details about the extent of the devastation, as if we were afraid to name things, lest our words result in a higher death toll.

Moreira was a tall man, with long, unkempt gray hair and moles on his face. He wore various shades of brown. Although he had given up smoking, he retained the habits of a heavy smoker. He put his fingers to his lips, as if he was inhaling a dose of memory or conversing with time. A painful silence lingered over the table after the first mentions of Lisbon. I didn't know what to say, so I looked around me. "You have so many books, Moreira!" My comment brought him out of his reverie. A smile spread across his face. In his usual crude but wise way of putting things, he paraphrased a strange aphorism: "A Homer or a Milton can have the same force as a comet colliding with the earth." He got up, looked for a book on the shelf, opened it, found the fragment he had just recited, and read the original in Portuguese. He said, "Everything has been written, Fernando. Senhor Pessoa knew it and that's why he wrote it down here, in his treatise on saudade. Oh, Lisbon! My beloved Lisbon. What sin might we have committed to deserve such misfortune? I grieve for Lourenço and Teolinda. I wonder what happened to them. Could they have survived? Would they have felt any pain? It's ironic, isn't it? They fled this country to escape death, but misfortune followed them to their new home." I didn't know the people he was referring to. Moreira's eyes were fixed on the closed door at the back of the living room. "I'm glad that Agustina can't understand what's happening. Her conscience, her bad conscience, could not bear it." He downed a glass of wine, and his tone changed. "How's the theater?" he asked. I lied. I reeled off a few platitudes about the good of our theater group. "Those kids need you, Fernando. They have to finish the play." I hadn't thought about it, but I was meeting the kids at La

Sibila later that afternoon, to resume rehearsals and ask them if they wanted to continue with the play. I still hadn't come back down to earth from the aftershock of what had happened. A stomach-churning nausea swept over me. For a moment, I experienced a vivid image of the destruction of the world. The Abreu brothers, missing in Lisbon, smashed to pieces. Marcel Hidalgo, the student imprisoned in notorious La Tumba prison, surged into my mind. Amid the howls and screams of a protest outside came the voice of my aunt, conjugating an irregular verb. The distant sound of a shotgun blast triggered a panic attack in me. Casting aside my embarrassment, unable to contain my emotions, I burst into tears at the table. I didn't know what had come over me. I can usually control my actions, but in that quiet conversation, I fell apart. I felt ashamed in front of Moreira. I realized there was more to my breaking down like that than just the destruction of Lisbon. My nerves had been shot for months. For some time now, I had suffered sleepless nights, plagued by anxiety. And every morning, I was assaulted by the images of the kids being massacred on the highway, the widespread famine, the rampant misery, and Tatiana's patent lack of affection. It took one part of the planet to go up in flames for me to realize that my life, my insignificant life, was like that of a sad clown. Embarrassed by my show of emotion, I tried to make a joke of it. I pointed out the irony of the situation that I had come to visit him with the intention of consoling him yet he was the one who ended up consoling me. That unexpected conversation became a confession. For the first time in forty-three years, I dared to say that my life had no meaning, that my wife had stopped loving me, that I didn't know what I was doing in the classroom, that I lived in daily fear of my students being arrested or killed, while powerless to do anything about it. I bemoaned my apathy, my helplessness, my uselessness. I wrote myself off as a hopeless case, as a person with nothing to live for. Moreira listened patiently and attentively to my pathetic fit of self-flagellation. It took me a while to regain my composure. He offered me water. He said nothing. He just sat there, looking out the window. I felt as if I was being a nuisance, as if he was hoping I would leave as soon as possible. "I disagree, Fernando. In dark times, kindness is a rare commodity. I know that you are a kind person, who, like many others, has suffered many misfortunes. Allow me to tell you something: when we arrived in Venezuela, the abundance seemed inexhaustible. This country, my boy, had much to offer, and gave us so much. It wasn't easy, because it's never easy to start a new life elsewhere, but all those who had the will and determination to get ahead had found paradise. I'm not exaggerating or lying. I want to make you a proposition, Fernando. Do me a favor, and you will see how, after humoring me, you will look at your supposed misfortunes in a different light. You will come to understand some things better, and you won't be so hard on yourself about your past. What do you say?" Whatever proposition he had in mind, I could hardly refuse him. I nodded in agreement, thinking he was setting a trap for me. He took his time in replying: "Let me tell you my story. Let me tell you about the unexpected events that brought me here, to this country, to this city, and to Colinas de Bello Monte. Never underestimate the connections between people's lives. Sometimes, a person's life can tell us many things about our own existence. But it's late now, my good friend. The kids are waiting for you. Talk to them. Convince them they should do the play, and come back soon. Let me heal you with my memories of the past, and with your kind interest, help me bear my saudade for my dead homeland, destroyed by God, for reasons he will never share with us."

• • •

Reality struck at La Sibila, closing down the workshops, canceling the courses, and burning down the small library. The tear gas bomb, hurled through the second floor window in some losing battle, also destroyed the classic Encyclopedia Salvat collection donated by Ascanio. Most of the teachers left the country. The equipment was looted to be used in the *guarimbas*, the street barricades and roadblocks in protest against the regime. We had no chalk, no paint, no musical instruments, and no toys to support children's activities. The theater group survived by the sheer stubbornness of the kids, who refused to give up one of the few oases of their freedom. The La Sibila Cultural Center was a civilian, non-profit organization. For the past three years, it had offered a modest cultural program for the young people of Colinas de Bello Monte. Old Moreira put up the starting capital and set up its headquarters in an abandoned house on Avenida Chama, near the Sieng Sieng Chinese restaurant. After a short interview, filled with literary quotes and thoughts about the future, the enigmatic Portuguese man laid down a few conditions. Moreira would provide funds if I gave him a verbal commitment to take on the direction of the center, maintain its upkeep, and call it "La Sibila." Moreira's appearance was timely, almost miraculous. My romantic notion of setting up an educational arts space for young people in Caracas had suffered several setbacks. The Baruta Municipality knew about our project, but its support was sporadic. Backed by impressive PowerPoint presentations (put together by an ex-student, now studying IT at Central University), we presented business plans to supposed financiers, who didn't stop yawning throughout the presentation that led nowhere. When Carmelo, my partner and fellow pipe-dreamer pal from the Instituto Pedagógico Teachers College, was murdered during a robbery, I lost all hope and enthusiasm. He was killed one night after having a few beers at La Buhardilla and dropping friends off in El Rosal. On the day of his funeral, in the vast solitude of the Cementerio del Este, I gave up my dream of leaving behind a legacy. Caracas was ablaze with protests once again. The toll of dead and injured fanned the flames of resistance, and in turn, the repression became increasingly aggressive. The van that transported Carmelo's body to the cemetery had to navigate around several *guarimbas*. The roadblocks were guarded by angry hellhounds, with little compassion for those who needed to get past. Desperation made them aggressive and irrational. No one accompanied Carmelo's body; the cemetery staff helped me place the coffin in the grave. A feeling of desolation forced me to take painful stock of myself and weigh up the worth of devoting my life to shaping the minds of future of generations, who were in general ungrateful and indifferent to our fate. I forgot about the cultural arts project and went back to just teaching high school. And then, when I least expected it, Giménez informed me that an old Portuguese man, who lived in the Centro Polo building and who had lunch at his bar on weekends, had heard about my plans and wanted to make me a proposition.

• • •

I was surprised they had all shown up. Considering what

was happening on the other side of the world, weighted with the uneasy expectation of impending aftershocks, I thought we would have to suspend rehearsals. But there they all were. The kids were sitting in a circle, talking quietly among themselves, a stark contrast to the usual noise of their banter at the late-afternoon rehearsal meetings. They looked at me as if waiting for me to tell them something important, as if I had the answers to the unsolvable riddles of the universe, as if my words were capable of allaying their uncertainties or convincing them that everything would turn out all right and that what happened in Lisbon would not affect us. They didn't know that my inner life was a disaster and that my insecurities barely masked my sense of defeat. "Good afternoon." I sat down on the low patio wall. Little Jacobo was drawing in his notebook. He seemed to be coloring a fire. The members of the theater group were senior year students from various highs schools in the municipality, from ninth grade and upward. But Jacobo was only in seventh grade. I didn't like working with the junior kids. Whenever we accepted them into the program, inevitably they would leave the workshop after the second week, bored and unmotivated. But Jacobo's determination to become an artist made him an honorary member of the crew. On the day of his interview, he told me he was the best actor in Venezuela and that if we let him go we would regret it. He started out with minor roles and helped make the sets. He went on to gain a place in the group, acquiring new responsibilities through his versatility and talent. He was tiny, and had a sharp childish voice, but he was overflowing with energy. He liked to rap, to make percussive sounds with his mouth, and to compose protest songs that contained swearwords and obscene adjectives. During the protests, he dressed as a superhero. He looked like an Anopheles mosquito, with a white shirt covering his face, a tin breastplate with a Deadpool logo on it, and a faded flag tied around his waist. He was afraid of nothing. He would pick up the (hot, heavy) tear gas canisters by hand and throw them back at the armored vehicles, goading the drivers to take them away. In Richard III, the last production we put on before the center was shut down, Jacobo played several roles, but his favorite was that of Clarence's murderer. I missed Marcel. I knew they all missed Marcel. His family still had no word on his condition. They wouldn't let them see him. Before the digital media blackout, the rumor was that he was being held in La Tumba and that he was being subjected to the "white room torture." Marcel was the one who chose Shakespeare's play. A week before he was arrested, he convinced the group that our next production had to be *Richard III*. I liked to let them choose, to present them with alternatives of classic works of drama, and then to let them decide which one they wanted to do. "Nothing avant-garde," Moreira had said in our verbal agreement, following the example of a man named Romeo. "Before they can set fire to the stage, turn their backs to the audience, relieve themselves in public, or display tasteless and irreverent humor, first they need to know the classics. If they stay on in the group, they will have time to try out their own ideas and to turn their unruliness into art." The first year we did *A Midsummer Night's Dream*. But the most recent group of students (Marcel, Mimi, Jeanco) had shown more interest in political theater, in protest disguised as theater. We started by doing *Mother Courage and Her Children*, and the following year, *An Enemy of the People*, with a superb Marcel in the role of Dr. Stockmann. Despite my many years as a teacher and my experience with hundreds of students, I find it hard to explain the phenomenon of leadership. I find it curious how some kids can naturally win over and influence their peers. Marcel had that mystique, that charisma. He wasn't a great actor. His acting was affected and unnatural, but he enjoyed what he did. The aim of La Sibila was never to train theater professionals. I wasn't qualified to teach acting. My only intention was to guide them, to distract them, to keep them off the streets, to awaken a passion or interest in them for something other than fighting. We put on two productions per year, the first in April, before Easter, and the second at the end of the school year, after the exams. We sold tickets for next to nothing at all the neighboring schools, and dropped flyers (designed by Jacobo) at La Buhardilla, Sieng Sieng, and Giménez's bar. We didn't make money out of it, just enough to barely pay for the maintenance of the center. But we were left with a feeling of immense satisfaction, and the people of Colinas de Bello Monte were grateful to see the kids engaged in a healthy and harmless diversion, without the latent fear (at least for the duration of the performance) that a burst of shrapnel would end their lives, or that they would be beaten up and hauled off to El Helicoide prison. After they arrested Marcel, we decided to go on with the play. We owed it to him, the group said. The issue was that we had lost our main protagonist. When Mimi said she would take on the role of Richard, I liked the idea. Within my limited knowledge of literary history, I was not aware of any woman having played the Shakespearean villain before. Mimi was a girl with boundless energy. She was in her final year at Promesas Patrias High School, and was relentlessly watched over by her inexpressive boyfriend, Román. She had curly brown hair that always looked shiny.

In Marcel's absence, she had emerged as the spokesperson for the group. The kids were devastated by the events of Lisbon and were afraid something similar would happen in Caracas. They needed a Virgil to guide them through hell, but I wasn't a poet and nor had I written any epic verses. "Hey, Teach! Is the world going to end?" she asked calmly, with a smile on her face. "I don't know, Mimi," I said, shrugging. "Cool," said Jeanco, getting up and tapping his belly like a drum. They kept their eyes on me, waiting to hear some soothing words. Esteban and José Luis, with their arms wrapped around each other, stared at me from a broken desk. Andrea challenged me with her blank, timid expression. The buzz of insects broke the pervasive silence. The energy saving light bulbs gave our faces a ghastly pallor, as if we were a group of sick puppets instead of actors in a theater workshop.

Esteban and José Luis were a couple. Their relationship was a scandal that went viral and almost cost them their place at Santo Tomás de Villanueva, a Catholic high school. The false rumor that a teacher had caught two students in the act of having sex in the bathroom became a hot topic of conversation during breaks. There was supposedly a video of them doing it too. I never saw it, but the students across all levels spoke about the details of the sex act with derision and malice. The girls all thought José Luis Álvarez was the handsomest guy in the Baruta Municipality, and said it was such a waste that he was gay. At the same time, his effeminacy offended their notions of how a man should be. From what Julia told me, the infamous video, in which all you could see were the silhouettes of two people hugging, prompted emergency meetings and in-depth staff discussions. While the country was falling to pieces and the city had become a minefield, the school was vehemently debating the question of how they should be appropriately punished. The young lovers became a target for people's collective frustration, people on whom they could unleash their feelings of powerlessness. The most hardline ones professed their outrage at what they considered unacceptable behavior. They gave the boys hell, humiliating them to the point of tears, laying into them daily, and turning their profile photos into satirical memes. La Sibila was a safe haven for them. Marcel, who'd been expelled from Santo Tomás de Villanueva years ago, stood up for them. Mimi and Jean Carlo offered them honest and non-judgmental support. Their relationship didn't bother anyone in the theater group. They gained confidence, and demonstrated their skills and talents. Within a few months, the scandal had blown over. Everyday problems and the advent of the conflict took precedence over people compiling dossiers on the young boys in love.

"There is no explanation for what happened." At last, I found the thread. I felt capable of putting forth an argument. I've never been able to understand the clarity and power of expression I find in the classroom. I'm usually awkward and erratic, even a bit gaga at times. I have a limited vocabulary, full of fillers like "I mean" and "you know." I don't think I'm very smart, but when I stand up in front of a group of young people, when I play the role of moderator in class discussions, I become a consummate speaker, almost erudite. What I don't know, I make up. Oddly enough, later on, when I look up the information to confirm my hunches, I realize that those random statements I made were in fact true. Outside the classroom, among people my own age, and faced with the harshness of the real world, I don't have much to say. But inside the classroom, I'm a gifted teacher. I say this without modesty. I like my work and I feel I do it well. My Aunt Rosaura's example has stuck with me: tone of voice, pausing, tempo, intonation, even the hand gestures that accompany each lesson, are all-important, as if the exercise of teaching was an act of elegant choreography rather than the sharing of knowledge. "Was Joaquín in Lisbon?" asked José Luis, referring to the youngest of the Abreu brothers, whom he'd studied with until ninth grade, and who had been the one who'd bullied him the most. We all knew the answer. He did too. He just asked the question out loud to try to get his head around it. So then I spoke to them about fear, fear of the unknown and the fragility of human lives. My ordinary comments became aphorisms. I told them they could ask any questions they wanted. Little Jacobo responded with his usual rancor, condemning God's will. "Why Portugal? Wouldn't it have been better if, instead of wiping out Europe, that meteorite had crashed into this shitty country?" "We should give thanks to God," Esteban insisted, interrupting Jacobo's rant. Furious, Mimi condemned Esteban's naivety, his blind faith and his stupid beliefs. Tempers flew. I let them face off, have it out, and abuse the Spanish language. Most of my students had a limited vocabulary. Their communication consisted of silly interjections, shortened words, and profanities. They didn't need anything else. With just four or five words, they had absolute mastery of the language. In the teachers' lounge, my colleagues railed in mock horror against the daily slaughter of the language, indignantly claiming that technology was perverting the younger generations, as if they themselves were somehow safe from it. I can't demand of the kids what we haven't given them. I can't ask them to analyze the syntax of sentences that mean nothing to them, when they don't know the sense of the language. I can't judge those who decide to leave, those who drop out of school because they consider it a waste of time. But I can recognize the value of those who, despite having everything against them, are interested in theater, cinema, or poetry workshops (shut down more than two months ago because, at a rally in Chacaíto, intelligence officers from SEBIN (the Bolivarian National Intelligence Service) arrested the teacher, accusing him of inciting violence). My question about whether we should go on with the production or not forced them to sign an armistice. Jean Carlo was the first to speak. "Let's keep going," he said quietly. "Let's do the play, what the fuck. If the damn world's gonna end, then let it end there," he said, pointing at the stage. The kids trusted me because I never talked down to them. I didn't treat them like idiots. I didn't harp on the poverty of their vocabulary. I let them swear, because I knew that was the only way they knew how to express themselves. Over the years, I've heard many wild and implausible stories from hundreds of students. I think they told me their stories because they felt comfortable with me, and because, unlike many of my colleagues, they knew I wasn't going to condemn them or smugly tell them how to live their lives.

Esteban gave out copies of the script, calling on the others to rehearse the scene with the ghosts. There was only a month to go before opening night and there was a lot of work to be done. It was the same every year. In the weeks leading up to the performance, it looked as if we wouldn't be able to pull it off, that it would be impossible to be ready on time. But in the end, we managed to put on the production, unpolished, without a budget, with homemade props, without batteries for the flashlights to produce stagy effects, but with the honesty of those who believe in the intrinsic value of their efforts. After rehearsals, we closed the security gate. We all left together. It was dangerous to go out alone, especially for the girls. Jeanco, affectionately known as "Gordo" because of his weight, lived in my building, on a bend in Avenida Casiquiare. We accompanied the others back to their houses and then walked home together, talking about his favorite subject, movies. All sense of calm flew out the window on the return home. The peace I had found at La Sibila was shaken when I realized I had to face Tatiana again. The image of my hostile wife, the aggressive woman who seemed to want to kill me, was at odds with the girl who not that long ago was so in love with me. I couldn't imagine losing her, but I suspected that saving our marriage was a pipe dream. As hard as I try, I can't pinpoint the moment we grew apart, the moment we stopped being close. I can't find a specific point in time. I have a feeling it happened during the protests. In particular, the protest where many people had to swim across the polluted Guaire River while being pursued by National Guard troops. My agoraphobia (the sound of a shotgun blast in my eardrum) forced me to stay in Colinas de Bello Monte, near the Central Madeirense supermarket. But Tati walked to the highway with Yolanda and some other friends from the optometry shop where she worked. The protest was met with disproportionate force. The following night, after an anguished-filled day, I found her in the Domingo Luciani hospital. She had an eye infection: her cornea and retina had turned a yellowish color. There were no antibiotics available to treat the infection. We had lost the battle once again. The tyrants had held on to power, contributing to our demoralization. I don't know if it happened then, I can't be sure, but I think something in Tatiana died that afternoon, suffocated by excrement, her lungs flooded with shit. At home in bed, she turned into a lifeless automaton, a cold, unfeeling doll, who didn't look at me in the same way anymore. When we reached Jeanco's house, I went in with him and said hi to his mom. Señora Hernández kissed the top of Jeanco's head, as if he were a small child. She offered me a glass of lemonade, and recounted the apocalyptic rumors she had heard while waiting in line at the broken-down ATMs. She thanked me for keeping Gordo company, for giving him hope in the midst of nothing. I opened the door. Tati was ironing a shirt. The romantic feelings stirred by the tragedy had dissipated. Once again, I had become a drag for her. She didn't look at me when I came in. I went up to her and kissed her on the cheek, on her cold cheek. "How was your day?" She threw me a dirty look. "Not so good. The power was out at the mall. We couldn't open the shop. And yours?" she added out of politeness, just to say something, to maintain the charade of a healthy marriage. "Fine." I sat down on the sofa and kicked off my shoes. "The kids decided to continue with the play." I couldn't help but smile, feeling good about the theater group in the midst of so much unrest. She snorted in disgust. She turned off the iron, shaking her head. She looked at me incredulously, with utter contempt in her eyes: "For fuck's sake, Fernando! The world is ending and the only thing you care about is that your kids are going to put on a fucking play." She locked herself in the bathroom and didn't come out until midnight. She slept with her back turned to me.

Allegro

THE REST OF LATIN America was far less equipped to come to terms with the destruction of Portugal than we were. We knew how to live among ruins, without it being an inconvenience. Scarcity was so commonplace that it was rooted in our DNA as Venezuelans. The fear of something happening to us or the high chance of being attacked and murdered at night were like ingrained traits, unalterable laws of physics. Empty supermarket shelves didn't shock us. We were no strangers to shortages. The crises in neighboring economies was a stage we had already gone through, a harmless plague that we survived without any vaccines or traumas. After Lisbon, only two things changed in Venezuela: total disconnection from the rest of the world (complete control of the internet by SEBIN) and the disappearance of the sun behind a mass of metallic clouds that settled over the Caribbean. In those first few weeks, there was a collective anxiety. The loss of access to social media was likened to genocide. It was the absence of leisure-time activities, rather than the reports of the catastrophe, that caused mass depression. Free time was an affront, a threat to the inner peace of those downcast spirits, for whom Facebook, Instagram, and Twitter were the ideal social masquerade. People had no clue how to navigate their way through life without the advice of the most popular influencers. My outdated phone kept me safe. The only app I knew how to use was WhatsApp, and only because Tatiana had insisted on installing it for me. The effects of the separation from the virtual world were alarmingly noticeable, especially in young people. Without a phone, they looked autistic, like zombies, or as if they were terminally ill. The possibility that we might never connect to the web again seemed more alarming than the disappearance of the sun, which was regarded as a minor problem in comparison.

The absence of information led to all kinds of absurd speculations. For those with relatives in Europe, the uncertainty was devastating. After a period of ritualistic mourning, the state TV channel began to spin elaborate conspiracy theories. The evidence, they said, was overwhelming: officials from the American embassy in Lisbon had been evacuated unexpectedly two days before the disaster. The president of Portugal was not at the São Bento Palace. That morning he had moved with his family to Sweden, claiming he needed to attend some trivial forum on ecology. The great villains, in the opinion of the official version, were the European Union, the United States, and NASA, who, despite having the necessary scientific data to anticipate the impact, agreed to remain silent and offer up ancient Lisbon as a sacrifice. This natural (or divine) occurrence was interpreted by the revolutionary "intelligentsia" as an act of sabotage, as a desperate strategy for ailing capitalism to exploit new markets by creating a cataclysm. Information about what really happened, which some journalists managed to obtain through clandestine channels, was much harder to stomach. The devastation was absolute. Lisbon was a crater. Much of the Iberian Peninsula had been razed by the curtain of fire. Day after day, there were earthquakes and debris storms. Floods had devastated the Galician and Aquitaine coasts. The heat scorched all life, turning green into cobalt, fields into deserts, and mountain ranges into craggy slopes. As in the times of the world wars, listening to foreign radio was our best means of finding out what was actually going on, better than restating word-for-word something that a lot of unintelligent commentators said: the theory that the asteroid that struck Portugal had been developed in the basements of the Pentagon.

Richard III was one of the best productions we put on at La Sibila. The staging was spare, without the sophisticated sets of the original, which were out of the question for our budget. Jacobo and Andrea played multiple roles, including extras and victims of the tyrant. Mimi was tremendous. The lighting effects produced by lanterns and blurry spotlights gave her foam rubber hump a sinister look. She delivered her lines confidently and with authority. She had a good grasp of the ethical dimension of the character and the rhetoric of his speech, which corresponded to the perverted reality of us Venezuelans. The audience held its breath every time she came out on stage. There were no annoying cell phones going off at inopportune times or screens glowing in the darkened rows. The story of the ruthless and arrogant man, who usurped the throne of England with devious, underhanded tactics, was like a jolt to the passive audience, demoralized after the continuous suppression of the protests on the Francisco Fajardo Highway. Marcel's choice was right. The play was a success. The previous year, inspired by the Skena theater group, we put on *An Enemy of the People*. But even though the text was studded with sly nods to our own oppression, the audience did not really connect with the play, not in the way they did with *Richard III*. Mimi's performance had a lot to do with it. A Richard played by Marcel would not have had the same deep impact. Tati did not attend the premiere; I waited for her at the door. I missed the beginning of the performance, but I was confident in the group's ability to pull off the first act without the need for a prompt. They were all up to it. Jacobo, dressed as a medieval soldier, an egomaniacal feudal lord, or a messenger bearing bad news, lightened the drama. Comedy was his forte. His mere presence on the stage had the effect of a joke. Andrea had covered up her tattoo with makeup. Queen Margaret's curses broke the fourth wall and shook up an otherwise impassive audience. I had known Andrea since eighth grade. She was soft spoken and lacked confidence. She found it difficult to come out of her shell. At school during breaks, she didn't dare go to the cafeteria with the others. She was afraid of being misheard and making a fool of herself, or worse, that no one would even notice her. The theater, however, took away her inhibitions. When she was on the stage, she came out of herself. "May conscience eat away at your soul constantly," she cursed Richard. "Fuck!" Giménez shouted in the second row, babbling something in Wong's ear. "May you never sleep a wink except to dream of a hell full of ugly devils." Esteban and José Luis also did their part, playing conflicted murderers suffering pangs of conscience as perpetrators.

And then, to bolster our small share of pride, Gordo Jeanco, my "little Orson Welles" as we used to call him, entered the stage. My kids were all good actors, but Jean Carlo was the best. He delivered his lines flawlessly, making his words seem spontaneous. The final scene was chilling. The lighting effect suggested by Román worked perfectly. The minimalist sets (forced minimalism, more than aesthetic) made the despot's fall even more pathetic. Mimi fell to the stage on her knees, her arms outstretched to heaven. "The battle is lost." And before slumping on the ground, in a broken voice and with a glassy stare, she said: "A horse, a horse, my kingdom for a horse!" Everybody in the audience stood to applaud. Even the usually inexpressive Giménez, with cigarette in mouth, cried out a raspy "Bravo!" After the ovation, I was invited up on stage. I squeezed in between Andrea and Jacobo, with a feeling of immense satisfaction for having been part of something good in the midst of so much ruin, scanning for Tati's face in the front-row seats. Mimi took off her hump and motioned to Gordo. He went behind the curtain and came back out with a banner, which they unfurled to read: "Freedom for Marcel." The euphoria grew, but the resentment on the faces in the third row did not go unnoticed. The condemnatory speeches in the play caught the attention of the anonymous censors sitting in the audience. We had gotten used to living among "patriotic informants," those who, despite having shared the same discontent and hardships over the years, reported to the authorities any hint of dissent. They didn't wear a uniform or look evil, but the slightest hint of rebellion was enough for them to accuse anyone of illegal activities (hoarding basic goods, trading in US dollars, *bachaqueo,* assassination plans). Many of them were our friends. I don't think they did what they did out of malice. They were desperate men and women who, in exchange for treatment at the Military Hospital or a food parcel from CLAP, dispensed with their "inviolable" dignity. I suspected there might be consequences in putting on the production. It wasn't the first time it had happened. The previous year, after *An Enemy of the People,* we received a notification from the Ministry of Education and Culture expressing concern about the mental health of young people being exposed to counterrevolutionary propaganda. The rhetoric of the text was overblown and contrived. They threatened us with the application of the Organic Law for the Protection of Children and Adolescents (LOPNA) and the Law Against Hatred. They warned us that our activities at La Sibila would be closely monitored, and recommended we remove from our courses any type of literature that could undermine the dignity of Venezuela. The same thing had happened to me at the high school, with Gordo as the protagonist. But I always imagined that those accusations would have no real effect, that they were just gross intimidations or ostentatious displays of aggression by resentful civil servants. I never thought they would keep their word, their cowardly word, and dare to close us down, under threat of a fine, prison, or death.

The most significant (and the strangest) confrontation with power occurred the previous year at Promesas Patrias, when the eleventh-grade group staged a performance of *The Divine Comedy*. The absurd farce took place in Principal Monagas's office. When I walked into the administration office, I came face-to-face with a representative from the Ministry of Education and a SEBIN official. They skipped the pleasantries and immediately asked me to give them "my version" of the events, but the truth is that nothing had happened. I didn't know what they were referring to. Despite saying they had credible witnesses and reliable evidence, it wasn't clear to me what crime had been committed in the classroom. They stated that, under my duty of care, some law or other called the Social Responsibility Law had been violated, assaulting the memory of the Eternal Commander and the dignity of the homeland. I wasn't afraid. The accusation made no sense. I just assumed the whole trivial episode would be dismissed as irrelevant. But a chill ran through me when the woman from the Ministry of Education took out a notebook and read out the full names of Andrea Echenausi and Jean Carlo Hernández.

My teaching philosophy was based on creative expression. I liked the kids to be inventive, to take the basics of the curriculum and transform it into something else. Not only did they have fun, but they would also take away a smattering of knowledge, because unlike many of my teaching colleagues, I knew that a high school diploma was only a shallow introduction to the world. They wouldn't be able to learn everything that the curriculum intended for them to learn. They just needed to find out what they were interested in, form their own tastes, so that later on they could decide what they wanted to do. Ordinary people often underestimate the responsibility of the teacher. Day in, day out, I have a duty to stimulate and maintain the motivation of a group of young people who have no interest in life, because the world around them has nothing to offer them. I have to look them in the eye and try to convince them there are things worth fighting for, even if I myself have stopped believing in those things. All my former students will remember, in more or less detail, my outlandish practical classroom activities: a zine made of cardboard with various images, texts, and messages relating to the Baroque era; a blog written by Don Quixote; a model of the Trojan War; promotional flyers about the Generation of 1928, the group of students who led protests in Caracas against the dictatorship of Juan Vincente Gómez. At the beginning of the year, in the seventh-grade class, at Jacobo's initiative we held a song contest in which García Lorca's poems were performed to the rhythm of bachata. When we studied *The Divine Comedy,* I came up with a strategy of dramatic reenactment. The kids worked in pairs. They had to select a scene from the book and present it to their classmates. I'd been doing this activity for six or seven years without any trouble. Most students chose a verse from *Inferno,* learned it parrot-fashion, and did the bare minimum to meet the requirement. They never chose something from *Paradise*. They didn't like it. Other students put all their efforts into the form, into the shabby costumes and flimsy sets painted in cartoon red flames with which they tried to turn the classroom into a sinister circle of hell. But the performances were disastrous. They giggled, failed to understand the substance of the text, and, without grasping its essence, returned to their desks, satisfied that they had obtained a sufficient grade. Andrea and Jean Carlo always worked together. Their friends said that Gordo had been in love with Andrea since preschool, but that he'd never dared to confess it. He disguised his attraction under a cloak of unconditional friendship. Andrea trusted him. I'd even go so far as to say he was her only friend, one of the few people who managed to break down her shyness. There were twenty minutes to go before the end of class. Their turn was last. Jean Carlo put on a brown cloak and wrapped a brightly colored scarf around his neck. Andrea was wearing a white jumpsuit.

With her hair up, the lizard tattoo on her neck gave her the appearance of a fallen angel, a rock fan. As soon as she came out and stood in front of the class, I knew it would be a special performance. Unlike the other pairs, Andrea and Jean Carlo had read the book and had something to say. She folded her hands in front of her and spoke with her eyes closed. "Now, young apprentice, we shall begin our tour through a parallel circle, about which there is no record in any version of *The Divine Comedy*." They mimicked Latin rhetoric, fooled around with highbrow vocabulary, and had fun with the language. "Come with me to explore this inhospitable territory, which some braggart called 'Little Venice.'" Nervous laughter rippled through the class. They had captured the class's attention. Jean Carlo came into the classroom and looked around apprehensively, wrapped up in his dirty cloak. Andrea walked in front of him. They moved in a circle, at a slow marching pace. The guide stopped suddenly. Gordo clung on to her desperately. He pointed to the wall. "Dear Master, you who keeps such a watchful eye over me, tell me please who those people are, buried in the mire, with sores over their bodies, submerged in that river of excrement, and who, despite being covered in honey and besieged by poisonous wasps, seem to be enjoying their suffering? Why are they laughing? Do the bites tickle them? Do they like smelling like shit?" Andrea raised her right arm and directed his gaze to the center of the classroom. "These degenerates are suffering but do not know it. They are condemned to suffer eternal pain without realizing it, convinced that bitterness is enjoyment and misery pleasure. Look at their eyes. As long as they continue under the spell of the beast, they will take no heed of their own suffering. Only when that voice of the most stupid, foolish, and despicable of all the men who inhabits this world is extinguished, will they feel the full pain of their wounds. The wasps' venom will paralyze their liver, and the stench will make them vomit over each other." "All these fools are looking at that giant figure in the background. I will move closer to get a better look." Jean Carlo walked to the middle of the room, grimacing with anger, doubt, and pent-up rage. His classmates could not contain their laughter. "Dear Master! Is that lump of shit, with a pus-filled wart on its forehead, and who doesn't stop talking to the walls—is it who I think it is?" Jeanco clenched his fists and screwed up his face. "Hold me back, master! I cannot contain the urge to climb up the rocks and give that soulless bastard a few kicks up the ass." Laughter. "Be patient, reckless young man. When things change in the world, that evil soul will have the greatest punishment. For now, he just feeds off the will of the unfortunate, those wretched souls mired in the pit of despair who follow him blindly. He talks without saying anything, enamoured of himself, convinced of the effectiveness of his own invocations, but he hasn't realized that there are other rules here. The Devil is having his fun with him, making him believe he can keep doing whatever he wants to. But the Devil is just building him up, convincing him that the underworld belongs to him, so that later on he can devour him with greater enjoyment. When everything he did falls apart, when the shit scum he left in charge of this city finally depart, when history turns his mercenaries into whimpering dogs, then his true ordeal will begin. The weak who worship him will stop laughing, and, in addition to feeling the pain of the burning stings over their bodies, they will realize that they are hungry. The beast will be devoured by its children. They will swarm over him like a mob of big, red-assed ants, sting him with their bites and scratches, then spew him back up and eat him again." "Dear Master, can I rip his wart off and take it home with me? I would like to spit and urinate on it daily or take it to Plaza Altamira and leave it at the mercy of an army of housewives." "Your action is noble, dear apprentice, but I guarantee you that you will not be able to coexist with that pestilence. Better to move on and ignore this unfortunate encounter. Don't waste your emotions on that which is not worth it. Leave things in the hands of God and Justice. They will take their time, but they will come. Some of those wretches who think they are untouchable will burn here. And I guarantee you that in the face of the Evil one's fury—the true Evil One—neither their arrogance, nor their rifles, nor their expired tear gas canisters will help them." Mimi stood up to applaud them, although some students remained silent. It was no secret we lived side by side with the children of aspiring political or military leaders. When Andrea and Jean Carlo put on that harmless performance, it didn't occur to me that it might lead to consequences. But there were some who were offended. The SEBIN official removed his dark glasses. I thought I recognized him. There was a familiar trait in his dead eyes, a vague and distant shadow I had long since lost sight of.

There is an Old Bello Monte on the other side of the Guaire River, distinct from Colinas de Bello Monte. Though the two adjacent neighborhoods share part of their name, the river demarcates the immense gulf between the inhabitants. The Los Gemelos Bridge, also known as Las Nalgas de Rómulo or Rómulo's Buttocks, delineates a frontier, a dangerous crossing. Everything in the area surrounding the El Recreo shopping mall is considered foreign to the inhabitants of Colinas de Bello Monte. The

Instituto Atenas was on the Bello Monte side, near Avenida Casanova. At one time, more than ten years ago, I worked there. I began as a substitute teacher and ended up staying on for a couple of years, until I got regular work at Santo Tomás de Villanueva, Promesas Patrias, and Fray Luis de León. The class differences between the inhabitants of the two Bello Montean neighborhoods were as uncomfortable as they were evident. The students at the Instituto Atenas were much more aggressive and completely disinterested. The task of gaining their attention and persuading them to shake off their apathy was more demanding. Teachers were enemies by nature. Attempts to get through to them fell on deaf ears. Alexander Soria, the SEBIN official who, years later, addressed me coldly in Principal Monagas's office, had been one of my first students. He looked like an old man. He seemed older than me. His adult self bore no resemblance to that sickly, lonely young kid from the Instituto Atenas. Alexander left school in ninth grade. He couldn't bear the bullying. He was beaten up the week before he left. Months later, I learned he had enlisted in the army. When I called him by his name, he was surprised. His memory wasn't as good as mine. I mentioned the old high school days. He forced a smile and seemed a bit put out that I had brought up those unhappy times. The juvenile remarks, the wisecracks, the relentless and crushing put-downs all came flooding back to me. I remember they called him Prepucio—Foreskin. His classmates made fun of him when they saw his tiny penis in the locker room after Phys Ed. The memory was interrupted by the woman from the Ministry. She asked me to tell her what had happened with the students, Hernández and Echenausi. Alexander's stern expression warned me to tell the truth and nothing but the truth. The woman held the notebook in her hand and wrote down everything I said. When I told her we were working on *The Divine Comedy,* she shook her head, repeating the word "comedy" to herself. "And what is it you teach?" "A bit of everything: history, art, literature." "Where did you graduate from?" Carlos Monagas stared at me blankly. "From the Instituto Pedagógico." "Years of experience?" "Nineteen, almost twenty." "And who gave you permission to call the Revolution a joke?" The stupidity of what she was saying contrasted with her hostile and heartless tone. I didn't know whether to laugh or be concerned. Her idle questions were aggressive and intimidating. I described the performance. I explained that the activity consisted of allowing the students to choose an episode from Dante's *The Divine Comedy*. She didn't stop taking notes. "Repeat the name." I sought Principal Monagas's moral support, but his eyes were fixed on the floor. "Dante who?" Silence. "The author of this piece of libel, what was his name?" "Alighieri," I spelled out. "Foreigner?" "Yes, Italian; a Florentine, actually. From the thirteenth century." Alexander scrutinized my reactions. The woman put away her notebook and informed me that the Ministry had received a complaint that a serious and unacceptable crime had been committed in one of my classes. The school would be fined, they notified Principal Monagas. Before they left, she urged me to reflect on my teaching practices. She said that I was free to hold whatever political views I wanted, but that I was not allowed to contaminate the free-thinking minds of defenseless adolescents with my prejudices and ignorance, and even less so, brainwash them with foreign literature that was offensive to Venezuela. Alexander left without saying a word. Principal Monagas asked me for discretion. He warned me not to expose the students to acts of extremity. He asked me to speak to Jean Carlo and Mimi, popular and natural leaders in the Humanities course at school, so that they would support us in our efforts to keep the school open.

• • •

"God enjoys games of strategy and none of us knows what our own role is." He overfilled the glass with wine. Moreira's hand shook, and he had to make an effort to hold the bottle. I went back to visit him out of courtesy, but I had no real interest in hearing his life story. I didn't care what he had to tell me. I imagined his need to share his past with me was an effect of his old age, a commitment entered into that I would find difficult to avoid. Moreira sensed my unease. He asked me not to be impatient. In his polite and gentlemanly manner, he explained that there are invisible threads weaving together our fates. In the end, I had nowhere else to go. My personal life was in ruins. The tension with Tati was more unbearable with each passing day. Schools were in chaos, especially Promesas Patrias, and rumors of its imminent closure circulated daily. The only peaceful place was La Sibila. After the productions, there usually followed a period of calm and natural withdrawal. The only person left at the house on Avenida Chama was the caretaker, Macario, with an unloaded shotgun slung over his shoulder to ward off the delinquents constantly on the prowl.

"The world began in the Serra do Marão, in the highlands of Trás-os-Montes," he said, sipping his wine. "We are fortunate to share a common birthplace with Senhor Torga. We mountain people have that privilege. But Senhor Torga was born in São Martinho de Anta, and I come from a much smaller village." I didn't know what to say. I didn't know the geographical or the literary references he alluded to. "I don't know what the fate of my land will be now. I have no more information than you about what happened. Pantera maintains with enthusiastic ignorance that Europe has completely disappeared. But my understanding is that this new 'flood' only devastated the center of Portugal. They say that Lisbon is a fiery pit, that a black cloud mass extends from the Alentejo region to Porto, with burning rocks raining down everywhere, and that barefooted crowds are crossing the border into Spain. But there is no mention of the Nogueira, Padrela, or Larouco mountains. Who knows? Maybe Santo Andrés Avelino saved us from misfortune and from the storm. Oh! Forgive my digression. It's difficult to ignore what is happening, not to think about the pain of loved ones or remember my wanderings around the Praça do Comércio, now gone. My world started in a small village, a hamlet on the outskirts of Gouvinhas. I come from humble origins. We did farm work and gathered chestnuts. Our destiny was preordained: we were servants and could aspire to no more. Senhor Torga already said it, 'he who is poor must endure.' And to be honest, Fernando, I never had problems with my servile fate. Those who wanted to escape our condition had only two ways open to them: the seminary or Latin America, the Church or adventure. But my faith was not so strong, nor did I have a reckless temperament. My arrival in this continent was an accident. Believe me when I say that at sixteen I didn't know a place called Venezuela existed. I wasn't the brightest spark. I was a man accustomed to manual labor, someone who'd barely learned the basics of mathematics, and then only to make sure no sly merchants cheated me. Allow me to tell you my story slowly, to savor the memory like a good wine, to let it sit and enjoy the flavor in the telling. My brothers were also condemned to inherit a trade, a destiny, a way of life. Silvinho and Lourenço, the two oldest, were the only ones who went to school and escaped our fate. It's understandable, there was another world beyond the Serra do Marão, other languages and other forms of life to tempt them. My brothers' daring condemned the rest of us, because my father said that nothing good was taught at school, and that it wasn't worth spending half a day learning about trivialities when at the end of the day there were so many mouths to feed. Ploughing and cultivating the land was the only thing that could guarantee us a living, keep us busy, and for that it wasn't necessary to learn useless things. Actually, we were happy. We were content with little because ambition and dreams were forged from other materials, and many of them, the most beautiful, had been made for others. The religious pilgrimages and *endoenças*, the Holy week processions, satisfied the imagination of the children. We had nothing, but we had everything. And if the departure of my brothers had not made me the forced firstborn, if I hadn't had to help my father in his work, I probably wouldn't have met the young girl Agustina, and I never would have left Trás-os-Montes and, after a hasty departure, come to the beautiful Port of La Guaira."

He walked over to the back room, opened the door and left it ajar. A medicinal smell hit me and I nearly gagged. He went to the bathroom. A few minutes later he returned to the table. "My father worked as a domestic for a person of respect, who over time would become a congressman for Vila Real. After my father suffered an accident that rendered his hand useless, he asked me to accompany him to the main house. I took on the cleaning work, but, after the first few weeks, I earned the respect of my employers, who at the time were good people. I drove the first car that came to Gouvinhas. People were astonished by that motor vehicle. They had never seen anything like it, apart from in the movies that Father Silva projected in the square, charging us three pennies to watch them. The Gomes family's social ascent meant a climb up the ladder for me, too. I started wearing a white jacket. I had just turned eighteen and had never left my town. And that's when I got married—when I was *forced* to get married. Oh, poor Lucía! What can have happened to her? Mountain weddings were an alliance or contract between the old families. Romance only leads to perdition, as Senhor Camilo Castelo Branco perceptively notes in his beautiful novel. Matters of the heart and living arrangements were left in the hands of the elders and had to be dealt with in a timely manner. Lucía also worked in the congressman's house, in the kitchen. One Sunday afternoon, our parents discussed the benefits of our union. Some months later, Senhor Gomes was the best man at our wedding. But affection, as I am sure you well know, cannot be forced. If there is no respect for the other, if you cannot summon an iota of sympathy, living with them on a daily basis can become a hell. And I'm not exaggerating when I say that, from the first night, Lucía made her contempt clear to me. I don't think she hated me. That woman was furious at the world. She was eaten up by envy and discontent, and angry at her misery. Sometimes she would spit into the *caldo verde* soup or cast spells while cooking Senhora Gomes's breakfast, cursing the family's good fortune. I had the responsibility of providing her with a child, but we didn't know how to go about it properly. No one talked about these things. It wasn't done. We had no instincts. We didn't like each other. We just imitated the movements of the animals in the field. We tried to mount each other as the beasts did, but our bodies had no symmetry. The truth is, we were afraid of the night, because when we were forced to play the role of husband and wife, all we felt was shame and physical pain. Senhor Gomes spent a lot of time in Vila Real. The trips along the old road were endless, and my absences from Gouvinhas were getting longer. In the town, it wasn't long before I was branded a laughing stock and became fodder for gossip at the feast day of the *Virgen de la Fresa*. I was a cuckold. Lucía had a lover and didn't care to hide it. Everyone knew she was cheating on me. My father called me aside. He was very concerned about what people were saying, about the damage to our family's honor, and the manifest degradation of my manhood. Senhor Gomes unwittingly provided us with a solution. It was something that happened suddenly and that allowed us to escape the gossip of the mountain. His political career was on the rise, and if he wanted to aspire to something better, he had to move to Lisbon. He asked Lucía and me to accompany him and his family, to settle in the capital with them. My father entrusted the salvation of my marriage to São Bartolomeu. 'Take care of your wife, offer her what she needs, force her to respect you, teach her who is boss, and give her a son.' But the truth is I felt nothing for Lucía, not even resentment, and the mere thought of taking a swim in her pond left me profoundly uninterested. Moving to Lisbon was an adventure full of fear and expectations. Beyond the Marão was an unknown universe, one I wasn't sure I would be able to adapt to. Senhor Gomes asked me to leave earlier, to drive his wife and young daughter a few weeks ahead of the planned departure, to help them settle in. On the day of their departure, I found a comic book on the car seat:

Pulcinella in Trás-os-Montes, I managed to spell out, with my limited knowledge. I liked the drawings, the puppets' features, the ambivalence of the illegible letters. I traced my fingers over the words, trying to capture them, wanting to figure out what they were saying. A childish voice leaned over my shoulder and, slowly, savoring the syllables, helped me decipher the puzzle. 'Moreira, read me that story.' I felt ashamed. I lowered my eyes. I would have liked to please her, but I had to tell her that I couldn't read. She knew how to read, she said, but she did it very slowly. She was learning how to read in school. She said that if I wanted to, she could teach me how to read when we got to Lisbon. 'Thank you very much, Miss Agustina. Thank you very much.' If someone had told me then that, years later, I would share the rest of my life with her, I would have told them they were crazy. But as I have already said, God's paths are more winding and uncertain than the old road in Cambres. It's late, Fernando. Night has fallen, and you know that we live surrounded by sneering devils. Come back soon. Take care. May God grant us a good evening."

• • •

Tatiana was my student at Santo Tomás de Villanueva, but our relationship began ten years after she graduated, when we ran into each other at a bar in Altamira. At school, she was pesky and flirtatious. I never took her attempts at seduction seriously because they always seemed like childish games to me, outbursts of adolescent irreverence. "Hey, Teach! Marry me," she once said, at the end of a history lesson. She was leaning back in her chair, with her legs wide open up on the desk, petite, small, inviting me with her amber eyes. I got distracted grading tests. "I don't think that would be a good idea," I replied without looking at her. "When you grow up, you'll find a better husband than me." Then I ignored her, showing complete disinterest in her daring proposal. Disdain worked. She gave up flirting and started throwing tantrums instead. Tatiana was beautiful, but my moral hang-ups kept me from thinking of her in a different way. Her school uniform nullified my instincts. She was off-limits, sexless, like the rest of her classmates. The lessons of the world, learned the hard way at home, under the stern guidance of my aunt Rosaura, had left an indelible mark on me. A sense of morality being the deepest one. Many of my colleagues thought I was gay, because whenever we met up at either La Buhardilla or Giménez's bar, I never took part in their crude conversations about the girls' looks. I felt uncomfortable when they undressed the girls with their eyes and turned them into objects of desire. I remember a Phys Ed teacher, later accused of sexual harassment, who boasted to his male colleagues of masturbating daily to the yearbook photos. The Seminarians were the worst. Pastoral training served as the perfect alibi for them to get away with seducing unsuspecting teenagers. I'm not an idiot (not much, anyway). I knew that Tati was just pushing the boundaries. She was very young. I started teaching when I was twenty-three, so there was always going to be the risk of temptation. She enticed me with her mischievous looks, with her natural charm, but I wasn't willing to risk my profession and my emotional stability for an affair with a young girl. I didn't need it. At school, Tatiana would greet me with kisses on the cheek and hug me unexpectedly in the corridors until I felt uncomfortable, making fun of my awkwardness with her friends. My indifference kept her at bay, though she tried hard to annoy me. Years later, laughing, we recalled some of her attempts at seducing me, like the time when we did a shared reading of *The Red and the Black*. I liked to read during breaks, while doing yard supervision, stopping the kids from smoking or making out behind the trees or starting fights. I had always been interested in Stendhal's book, but hadn't had time to read it. The pile of unread classics on my nightstand was huge. Most of them I didn't read. I didn't have the time. But in my first years of teaching, I had the vain ambition of becoming acquainted in depth with literature. For two weeks, I was captivated by the adventures of Julien Sorel. I had the Cátedra edition with a tattered yellow cover, which I bought at the Divulgación bookstore in the Los Chaguaramos shopping mall. One morning, Tati crashed into me coming down the stairs. She apologized absentmindedly, holding a book in her hands: *The Red and the Black*. "Teach, sorry!" she said, ignoring me. And then she continued on, as if she hadn't seen me. In the next class, during a group activity, I confronted her. I asked her about the plot of the novel, about the characters, about the meaning of the title. She knew I was teasing. Furious, she wouldn't speak to me for a whole week after that. Years later, after bumping into each other at the Greenwich bar and going back to my apartment afterward, naked and exhausted, we read a few fragments of the novel in bed together, as if it were one of the items of unfinished business left between us.

The chance meeting at the Greenwich bar happened after Carmelo was a no-show for a brainstorming session about starting a cultural center. I waited for him for an hour at Plaza Altamira, but the heat forced me to seek refuge at a nearby bar. We had opened up discussions with the Mayor of the Baruta Municipality about setting up a cultural center in Colinas de Bello Monte, but we were still developing the project. There was a lot of work ahead of us. Later, I learned that Carmelo's car had broken down in Chacaíto, and that he'd spent the afternoon looking for a tow-truck service that wouldn't scam him. I walked over to the Torre Británica high-rise, opposite the old cinema. I don't know why I picked the Greenwich. I don't know the bars in my city. Giménez's being the local bar is an exception. I saw the green door and went in. I ordered a beer. The heat was relentless. They were playing '90s music: "*La Flaca*" (the Thin Girl) by Jarabe de Palo. It wasn't crowded. It was still too early. She appeared out of nowhere. "Hi, Teach." Ten years or so had passed since our last meeting, when I handed her her high school diploma in the school auditorium. I fell in love on the spot, without resistance or shame. Tatiana came into my life at a moment of extreme world-weariness and vulnerability, when I was constantly questioning the meaning of my lonely existence. She was with some friends. I recognized Yolanda, also a former student. I invited them to have a drink. She sat next to me. We talked the whole afternoon. Her friends left. I felt good with her and I sensed that she was enjoying my company, too. She told me about her higher studies at the Catholic University and the optometry shop she managed at the Paseo Las Mercedes shopping mall. She spoke with complete confidence, fully aware of the hypnotic effect of her words. "Do you have a girlfriend, Teach?" "Don't call me 'Teach'." "You'll always be my 'Teach,' but okay: Fernando. Do you have a girlfriend?" I'd never had a girlfriend. I wasn't willing to give up my independence. Julia was the closest I'd come to having a partner, but I wasn't comfortable naming her. Tatiana knew her. Julia had also been one of her teachers. Julia and I were casual and somewhat reserved lovers. When emptiness gnawed at us, when we hated the world, we would meet up at a motel in El Rosal to soothe our misery. We didn't like each other and there was no sexual chemistry between us, but we insisted on wrapping our bodies around each other, taking in each other's acrid smells, swapping sweat and saliva, so we wouldn't feel so alone. Later, when we saw each other at school, we would avoid each other. We never talked about what happened, as if it had never occurred. We assumed it wouldn't happen again. But then a few months later, after much deliberation, we would end up degrading ourselves, loving each other without pleasure or affection. Until I met Tatiana, I'd never felt comfortable with a woman. My sexual orientation was never in question. I knew what I liked. But the experience I had accumulated up to that moment, in my thirties, hadn't given me any security or pleasure. I didn't even enjoy kissing. Wet lips and tongue sometimes just had an irritating effect. Midnight took us by surprise. Back in that not-so-distant Caracas, it was still okay to stay out late. Crime hadn't yet brought about the strict curfews that would come later, and the lights along the highway had not been completely turned off. The first kiss was gentle, delicious, innocent. I felt the touch of her tongue against my lips. It tasted of beer. She was dismissive of my overture, telling me that she'd been waiting more than two hours for me to kiss her. My next comment was unexpected. I said it without thinking. "Come and stay the night at my place." She replied with a laugh. "Okay, fine. Why not?" I was crazy about her after that night, addicted to her humor and her gorgeous body. It rained on the way back to my place. We kissed in the rain, like in the old movies. Touching her, discovering her skin, listening to her laugh, was the most revealing experience of true love, something I had never felt or believed possible. Tatiana penetrated my defenses, invaded my blood and my mind. She worked on my awkwardness. She taught me things. I discovered the immense satisfaction of pleasing her, of taking her to the limit, to the point of silly laughter, of disarming her completely. We couldn't stop making love. We were insatiable, raw, physical, romantic, corny, and pornographic. I had lost my shame and self-doubts. I had the impression that we had always been naked, facing each other, and that an immense paradise stretched around us, one in which we were allowed to eat from all the trees. "Move in with me." She accepted. Two weeks had passed since we had run into each other. I'm certain that what existed between us was real and indissoluble, but things changed. The wonder ended. It wasn't infinite as we had thought. We let it fade without even realizing it. The destruction of Lisbon brought us closer together for a few hours. But as the days passed, it sent us on different paths, until it killed me with anguish, despair, and, above all, jealousy.

Scherzo

THE DAY I DISCOVERED Tatiana's secret, the protests swelled. The crowds made my agoraphobia worse. I sought refuge in Giménez's bar, where, as on numerous other occasions, Ascanio said the Revolution's days were numbered. The most widespread attitude, however, was one of cynicism and skepticism. What happened in Lisbon made us invisible to the eyes of the world. Venezuela was not a priority for any international organization. The sole focus of world politics was to fix the planet and restore stability to a shattered hemisphere that was still coming out of the tail end of the pandemic. The tyrannies of poverty-stricken countries took a back seat. Joint efforts directed at the liberation of Venezuela before the disaster had been stymied by the asteroid strike. Aware that no one was watching them, security agencies lost all restraint. The use of force, including cold-blooded murder, was the most effective control policy of a Revolution that had gotten a second life. Without decrees or slogans, they resorted to instilling fear. I reproached myself for wallowing in self-pity and dwelling on my own problems. My own misery made me indifferent to the tragedy of the world. All I cared about was keeping Tati, keeping her by my side, asking her to tell me the truth. I needed reassurance that my jealousy was unwarranted and that, sooner rather than later, things would return to normal.

She was hiding something. I knew her well enough to know that. In the months before Lisbon, I began to notice her obsessive dependence on her phone. She was constantly chatting on WhatsApp, in theory with her friend Yolanda. I could sense her checking her phone in the middle of the night, and she was always taking it with her everywhere, even to the bathroom. Whenever I glanced at her or walked past her, she would become uncomfortable, and she would look away from her phone and pretend to be doing something else. I confirmed my suspicion that she was having an affair when I found her *carnet de la patria,* or Homeland card, on the kitchen table. She claimed she couldn't work without the internet, that necessity had forced her to make the sacrifice of applying for the government-issued smartcard ID. Weeks after the catastrophe, phone services were restored in the rest of the world. Large corporations soon reactivated their operations, looking for alternatives in the face of ruin and for ways to weather the economic storm in the wake of the asteroid strike in southwestern Europe. The Revolution, however, took advantage of the tragic circumstances to reinforce censorship. Access to the internet and social media was to be monitored by Conatel, the National Commission of Telecommunications. The reason was technical rather than political. The Lisbon incident, as claimed by the official party's broadsheet, had caused a breakdown in satellite communications that prevented the free restoration of the web. Thanks to the intelligence services of the Venezuelan government, explained the ministers in office, the use of the internet could be reactivated, but with severe limitations. To ensure the operation of the service, state surveillance was necessary. The *carnet de la patria* was a prerequisite for requesting access to Google. Tatiana was one of the many people who lined up in front of SAIME, the state service that provides ID cards and passports, to regain their connection to the world. I hadn't asked her for an explanation, but she seemed to want to convince me that she had sacrificed her political principles for work reasons. Technological alienation returned to the apartment and her phone became my most fierce adversary. At night, she would laugh to herself, looking at the screen. I pretended to sleep, even to snore, as I looked at her through half-open eyes, contemplating her beautiful laugh, which she hadn't shared with me in months. Sometimes, she would lock herself in the bathroom and emerge half an hour later with a cheerful expression on her face. I hadn't seen that look since the days when we were dating. One morning, while having a coffee, pretending to be indifferent, I paid attention as she typed the password into her phone. I managed to make out the first three digits: 963. I missed the rest, but the memory of an old conversation reminded me of something. Tatiana knew all my passwords. She had set up most of my online accounts. When she asked me what password I wanted to use, I would quote the names of literary characters or the titles of books. "Stendhal" was our shared password, the one we used for our joint accounts. "You're so clever, Fer. I don't have any imagination," she had said in bed one time, soaked with sweat. "If I make up a name, I'm sure to forget it. That's why I always use familiar things, like my ID number or my old phone numbers, from when I was a kid." I replayed the conversation in my mind, watching it live, as if it were a hologram. Tati had grown up with her parents in La Boyera. And I knew that La Boyera's area code was 963.

First chance I got, I walked over to Las Mercedes. Trash lined Avenida Miguel Ángel, and there were roadblocks on the corners. There was no public transport. The gates were open at Santo Tomás de Villanueva, but nobody was around. Sister Salcedo was the only person in the office. I lied. I claimed I was looking for information about the students to organize the graduation ceremony. I went into the student records room. I remembered the year Tatiana graduated. She completed her entire formal education at that school. It was hard to find her among the infinity of Garcías. I found her card. There she was in her school photo, with the same look, with her long hair. I read her full name. I saw the address of her house in La Boyera. I found the number. I didn't have to write it down. I memorized it. I ran back to the apartment, passing unguarded *guarimbas*. I heard the sound of the shower. Her phone was on the nightstand, charging. I yanked hard, until I pulled out the cable. I entered the password. The screen lit up immediately. The WhatsApp icon was on the bottom left. A squirt of piss escaped me, and I felt a wave of uncontrollable dizziness. My throat filled with bile. Tatiana's lover was named Óscar, and he was also a former student of mine.

• • •

"'When evening falls across our streets / And sullen melancholy fills the air, / The Tagus, the tang, the shadows and bustle / Bring me an absurd desire to suffer,'" Moreira recited, staring out at the leaden sunset, with traces of the smoke from the tear gas bombs tattooed on the window. "Although, with the permission of our good Cesário Verde, I think we could swap the Tagus with the Guaire River." He seemed to be waiting for me. I didn't tell him about my feelings of despair, but he sensed them. He opened a bottle of wine. I was grateful for his sympathy, because everything I had read that morning on Tatiana's cell phone made me sick to my stomach. "Senhora de Mello Breyner was right about what she said about the pain of love, which I think may make sense in places like Venezuela. Forgive my translation: 'Terror of loving you in such a fragile place as the world. / The pain of loving you in this place of imperfection, / Where everything shatters and silences us, / Where everything deceives us and keeps us apart.' I am sorry that you are distressed, Fernando, but remember that, despite the deception and the disappointment, the essence of the things we love still remains intact. You have a firm basis for hope, even if it seems that everything is lost. For us Portuguese, on the other hand, we are left without a home. I come from a country that has disappeared, young man. After everything that's happened, I have the burden of memory. Oh, such sadness! But right now, the world's troubles don't interest us. You came to tell me about your woes, and here I am interrupting you with humanity's sorrows. If you want to talk, I can listen to you. If you want to stay silent, I can accompany you." Moreira was a born speaker, an all-round storyteller. His words, his foreign accent, had a lilting musicality, with an immediate soothing effect. I was interested in only one thing: not thinking, wiping the explicit details of Tatiana's WhatsApp messages from my mind. "Poets are lucky, but the rest of us mortals have to learn to live with grief. Senhor Ruy Belo from São Joao da Ribeira says that the poet is the one who manages sadness wisely. The rest of us don't have that luck." "Tell me your story, Moreira. Go on. You haven't finished telling me how you got here." I needed to distract myself, to focus my attention on something else.

"My marriage was a sham. The situation with Lucía did not improve in Lisbon. The enchanting effect of the big city was short-lived. For the inhabitants of the Marão, for all those who came from Trás-os-Montes, Lisbon was the capital of the world. We weren't used to living in a place with so many people, where we didn't know the names of all those we ran into on the street. And we felt as if we had to adapt to the frenetic rhythm of everyday life if we didn't want to end up on the sidelines. It's funny, Fernando. The wise travelers tell us in their memoirs that compared with London or Paris, Lisbon was a rundown village. But for us it was the City of God, the only known example of the modern world. I became Senhor Urbano's right-hand man. During the course of my daily errands, I got to know all the nooks and crannies of the Chiado, all the shortcuts, the alleys, the forbidden places, and cheapest marketplaces. The Gomes household lived through happy moments, but tragedy does not discriminate. After years of good health, the Senhora's illness came on, which led to her slow and gradual death. There's a long history of the ailment that is consuming my Agustina in the women of her family. Her grandmother, Senhora Tavares, had also met the same fate. After a certain age, something takes hold and cripples their blood, their bones, and their faculties. Her mother's agony was a carbon copy. We watched her wither away, day by day. Something happens to their brain, some sort of malfunction.

When Agustina first started getting dizzy, we both knew what would come next, because we had experienced it up close. One cannot outwit heredity. She asked me to promise her two things, then a few hours later she took to her bed. But the Agustina of Lisbon has nothing to do with my wife. I would say they are two different people. She was a tireless and resolute young woman. When her mother became ill, Agustina was about eighteen and she had a fierce temper. Oh, what a temper she had! What a character! She had strength enough to swallow the world, but a series of unfortunate events led the world to swallow her instead. The innocent girl from the mountain became conceited and unfriendly. The manners of the city, of the girls of her own class, affected her innate sense of kindness. She always treated me with respect, but she liked to keep her distance. The spontaneous warmth and affection of the girl who wanted to teach me to read dissipated, and those first-time lessons on the sound of the vowels were lost, along with the *Pulcinella* comics. Lucía could not abide young Agustina's beauty or her high status in society. My wife took pleasure in the mistress's illness. She would stare at her with morbid fascination, fixating on her grimaces, taking great delight in the knowledge of her paralysis. It was then, faced with the evidence of her cruelty, that I began to feel contempt for Lucía. I cursed my bad luck. I counted the hours until I didn't have to see her and endure her rants. She condemned my lack of ambition, my voluntary slavery. In Lisbon, she had an affair with a tailor. But unlike what happened in the mountains, nobody cared. No one was interested in the cuckold's horns of a domestic servant, apart from some other cuckold, who would toss off a few snide remarks in the taverns of the Baixa.

"Our marriage enabled Lucía to leave home, to escape

her sad life in Gouvinhas. But when we arrived in Lisbon, a new obsession began to gnaw at her: Latin America. At that time, Fernando, there was no greater spell than the one cast by the words 'Latin America.' On the other side of the world, we could have what we never had, be what we could not be. But prosperity came with a price: having to leave our homeland. And I thought, under no circumstance could I ever leave the majesty of the Tagus, that 'Mediterranean in miniature' as Senhor Almeida Garrett puts it so well in his memoirs of his travels. Lucía said that if we stayed in Portugal, we would never rise above our status as employees, that it would be impossible for us to have something of our own, and that the day Senhor Urbano's misdeeds landed him in the Peniche Fortress, we would be left alone, empty-handed, and burdened with unpayable debts. My wife's claims were like a nagging whisper, but there was something to her concerns. At first I didn't want to see it, but the evidence was clear. It made me sad to realize what had happened, but when we arrived in the city, Senhor Urbano changed. Politics, Fernando, is the devil's work. Where money is involved, good intentions get sidelined. Honesty goes missing. I know that in the Marão, Senhor Urbano Gomes was a good man, full of dreams and honest ambitions. But in Lisbon, bad company and temptations to power led him to unwise actions. It's not for me to judge him. That is God's job, but the truth is I wasn't comfortable with many of the things that were happening. My boss was involved in real estate speculation, using his influence to favor some and ruin others. He had a mistress in Almada, too. Meanwhile, at home, the Senhora was wasting away, caught up in an irreversible sleep that devoured her from within." Moreira's gaze fell on the closed door. A sigh interrupted his account.

A sudden smile came over his face: "How easy it is to get lost in the depths of memory! The young Agustina had grown up. Stubborn, restless, and headstrong. She was a headache for her father because, like most young people of her time, she was eagerly awaiting the arrival of the Revolution. The young people of that time thought that things could be different, that the word 'freedom' could extend beyond our quiet strolls around the Rossio, that it was possible to have a life free of Salazar's vigilance. The young Agustina had inherited her father's lost virtue, and she did not hesitate to throw his contemptible behavior back in his face. The theater group at the University of Lisbon was a hotbed of fiery youths. They possessed banned books and trafficked in censored works. In reality, they were well-off children who detested the privileges of their own class and elevated poverty into a romantic virtue. They never went hungry, but this did not stop them from idealising the beggar on the street and his humble lot. Life for them was not life. Existence was just a set of strange catchwords, of class struggle and celebrating the proletariat. It's not that their intentions were malevolent. The young Agustina lacked any malice. But those young people had never had to work hard or sacrifice for anything. When they returned home, after spending hours reading proscribed authors and planning failed attacks against Salazar, they found a plate of food on the table waiting for them and a warm bed to rest their heads. Ah, youth! That moment in life when you think that nothing is more powerful than your dreams! This is what Senhor de Sena tells us in his novel *Sinais de Fogo* (Signs of Fire), a beautiful story. The young Agustina fell in love with the director of the theater group, a bearded provocateur named Arlindo. He was older than her, and married as well.

It was a passionate and intense affair. Love, however, was merely an adjunct to the struggle, to their commitment to the freedom of Portugal. The romance ended months later, when banal conversations turned to concrete action, to true acts of sabotage, to the mission of a living Revolution. It was then that the PIDE, the secret police, appeared and, in the most absurd and unforeseen way, Senhor Urbano's only daughter ended up becoming my wife.

"I had two brothers in Latin America: Silvinho and Lourenço. Brazil and Venezuela were empty words for me, distant lands far away, outlined on a map. The situation in the Gomes house—the Senhora's illness, the Senhor's downfall, the young daughter's political zeal, and Lucía's insistence on leaving Portugal—forced me to make a decision. I started knocking on doors that could help me take the leap. It wasn't easy. There were many regulations and costs in organizing to leave the country. We needed an employment contract or a letter of invitation from a family member with a permanent place of residence in the Promised Land. The Emigration Board was strict and the officials did not care if you wasted whole days waiting around, only for them to reject your application for unjustified causes or, without prior announcement, double the charge for the criminal history checks and the medical certificates. We were lucky. When we went to the municipal offices to request our passports, we were attended to by a kind person. We met all the criteria. My brother Lourenço had answered my call for help. He was in Caracas. He ran an events company and needed employees. I hadn't pinned my hopes on Lourenço. I thought my letter to him would go unanswered. My childhood memories were more deeply rooted with Silvinho, the eldest one, the person who taught me how to swim in the Sabor River, and with whom I used to play old-fashioned mountain games on Gouvinhas's summits. But it was Silvinho who never replied. The letter to Brazil went unanswered. I don't know what became of him. Oh, it's a sin what migration does to families!

"We would leave at once, without saying goodbye, without giving explanations. I didn't want to do it like that. I was sorry to leave Senhor Urbano in that way, with his ailing wife and his crazy daughter's secret plan to organize an insurrection. But there came a time when the relationship with my boss became intolerable. His wealth affected him. He only wanted to listen to himself and, to top it all off, he drowned his bad conscience in alcohol. During the last few months in Lisbon, I went about my everyday duties. The imminent departure intensified Lucía's hostility. She became even ruder and more aggressive. Her affair with the tailor was public knowledge. One time, she told me the first thing she would do when she got off the boat would be to find a real man, that she was only with me because I could offer her a passport, but that she regretted having to share her life with such a nobody. I never questioned my marriage. God blessed our union. We made a sacred vow at the altar to love each other forever, in sickness and in health, but we never loved each other and never would. God is wise. He made the world, yes, and the world . . . well, it's beautiful, but it also has its flaws. If he had taken his time, it would have been better. Lucia's betrayal didn't hurt me. I preferred she be in the arms of the tailor than at my side, cursing her luck or wishing evil upon a dying woman.

"The day our lives went awry, the lives of all those related to this story, I came upon Lucía and her lover in an alleyway in the Baixa. Chance caused me to stumble on them, without them realizing it. She looked like a different Lucía. The way she held her lover, the way she looked at him, the way she seemed to enjoy his closeness. I had never seen her like this before. That woman was happy. She knew how to smile. She knew how to get lost in an embrace. I never made her happy, even though, believe me, for a long time, I tried." I felt the prick of a tear. Half-remembered phrases from Tatiana's WhatsApp messages flashed through my mind, describing her shared ecstasy, the heat of her orgasms. "You can't beg for love, dear friend. As I said before, God may have united us in the church at Gouvinhas, but he lives up in the clouds where things are so much easier. The one who had to sleep with that woman was me. When I returned home, I learned the news: the theater had been raided. PIDE officers had arrested Arlindo, young Agustina, and several members of the group. The accusations were serious. They found weapons in the rehearsal room and plans to launch an attack on the port. What started out as an impromptu gathering concerning the imminence of the Revolution ended up becoming an urban guerrilla cell. And in their ignorance, in their clumsy idealism, they made so many mistakes, their leaders were subjected to fierce interrogation by the secret police.

"At that time, forced disappearances were frequent. People knew about them but kept quiet. Those who fell from grace could spend the rest of their lives in the Tarrafal prison camp on Santiago Island in Cape Verde, and life would go on without them, because under Salazar's reign, Portugal was servile and forgetful. We didn't like to make any noise. We knew how to be silent, to keep our eyes down and our backs turned. Those who'd been arrested, it was because they had done something, because they had asked for it. I didn't want to leave like this, with the uncertainty over the fate of the young Agustina. Lucía was overjoyed. She wanted Agustina to rot in prison so she could learn firsthand the true meaning of misery. Senhor Urbano faced a dilemma that could only lower him in the eyes of God. Between his family and his career, he chose the second option. He didn't intercede on Agustina's behalf. He didn't care. He stayed out of the judicial proceedings, because any intervention on his part would have involved a direct confrontation with Salazar and his ministers, and because, at that time, he aspired to a higher position in Congress. 'Moreira, that girl needs to be taught a lesson,' he said to me one day when she left the house. The young Agustina ended up alone, neglected by her parents, isolated from the rest of her comrades, and mistreated by angry PIDE officers. They hurt her, you know. She told me herself. You understand what I mean, don't you? They weren't nice to her—" He abruptly interrupted himself. "It's late, Fernando, you should go. I don't want you to have to walk home at night." He had trouble getting up, his leg had fallen asleep. He collected the glasses off the table and stood in front of the window, facing the gray horizon. "But, so that you don't remain curious, I will summarize the end of this episode. I will come back to this later, but for now all you need to know is that a PIDE officer secretly interceded on her behalf. He released her on one condition: that she leave Portugal immediately and not reveal anything about what had happened to her. I found her frantic and crying in the house, distraught at Arlindo's fate and indifferent to her own future, paralyzed by the trauma. The young Agustina had nowhere to go. If she wanted to preserve her life and her freedom, she had to leave Lisbon in seventy-two hours. My ship to Latin

America would be leaving in three days. I didn't think twice about it. I went over the documents. Lucía was twelve years older than Agustina, but they looked alike. The situation was desperate and demanded urgent action. I don't know how it occurred to me, I don't know why I said it, but it happened like this. You don't know how many times I have replayed that scene in my memory, surprised by my own determination: 'Miss, I have two tickets for passage to Latin America. If you want, you can come with me to Venezuela, at least until the heat blows over.' Agustina boarded the ship with Lucía's documents. One July morning, we left Lisbon. The departure of the Moreira couple was entered in the town records, despite the fact that we had never touched or seen each other with a look that went beyond affection. The ship set sail at dawn and, weeks later, after a long journey, in which we did not exchange a single word, we arrived at the port of La Guaira, transformed, for legal purposes, into husband and wife."

• • •

When both sides in the conflict signed an armistice, when the combatants took refuge in their homes and the military officers crashed, exhausted, on the floor of the arepa restaurants, a swarm of amorphous creatures emerged from the banks of the Guaire River. Somber, mutilated wretches (some missing arms or legs) went out in search of food. They huddled around the utility poles, tore open trash bags, and even ate the bags themselves. A vast mound of refuse stretched between Las Mercedes and the Bolivarian University. It was made up of food scraps from unsanitary restaurants and the negligible amount of trash produced by the impoverished residents. That night scene, however, was far more pleasant than the solitude of my room.

Tatiana had left. Confronted with the evidence of her deception, she gathered up a few things and took off. She didn't say anything. There were no impromptu explanations or justifications. Just silence. A deadly and unforgiving silence. Yolanda didn't know what to say to me. I got tired of asking her to talk to Tati, to tell her that I needed to speak to her. Our relationship was distant and formal. Even though she had been maid of honor at my wedding, she never stopped calling me "Teach." Madness gripped me. I took off my belt and wrapped it around my neck, ready to hang myself from a light fixture. The early hours were torture because, added to the disorienting silence of the morning, my head kept re-creating the episodes described in the WhatsApp chats. I didn't recognize Tatiana in those messages. She and Óscar had been indulging in sexual perversion. She reveled in lust, taking pleasure in crude and rough subjugation, asking him to pull her hair, to push her head, and suffocate her with his sex, to fill her throat with cum. They exchanged photos. I found a dozen images of an erect penis dripping with semen, accompanied by smiling emojis. The image of Tatiana's tiny body surfaced in my mind, framed in our bathroom, with my toothbrush and her perfume and the cracked tile in the background. If it were all just an act of imagination, my grief would not have been so deep. But Tatiana and Óscar discussed real encounters, talked about things that had happened between them and that they wanted to happen again. My manhood came apart, it could not recover from the blow, because my sex life with Tatiana had never reached the heights of pleasure she shared with her young lover. Their messages full of lust, the level of detail, the manifest pleasure, all of it made me think that our acts of love barely managed to excite her, that my devotion just made her laugh. I knew Tatiana was precious, something to be jealously guarded and kept safe. I always treated her delicately, with great care, as if she might break. But Óscar offered her a savageness that she seemed to like and that she begged for. I ran around the apartment with the belt tied around my neck, trying to drive out their stabbing words, just as in the early mornings I used to scare away the buzzing mosquitoes. That wasn't her. Those weren't her words. That wasn't her way of being intimate. *I want you in my mouth. Let me make you cum*.

The emails were over six months old. Tatiana and Óscar had run into each other during the protests, in one of the marches on the highway. They fled the repression and took refuge in an apartment. Their first chats were friendly and exploratory. I knew they'd had a high school fling, an unfinished story. "I want you to come to my house. We have some unfinished business to attend to," he wrote. I remembered the date. That afternoon, Tati told me she had an appointment with the dentist. Agony led to self-reproach. I regretted checking her phone and finding out. Even if we didn't talk to each other, even if she turned her back to me in bed and locked herself in the bathroom to send photos to her lover, I needed to have her close, to feel that she was there—mentally elsewhere, but physically by my side.

I read the chats and emails only once, sitting on the floor while she was taking a shower. After the fake dentist appointment, they started seeing each other once a week. Then at night, on WhatsApp, they relived what they had done and posed new challenges for themselves. They shared intense emotions, they swapped notes on the positions they liked, links to porn clips and of couples doing kinky things.

She always told me she was with Yolanda, but from what I read, her best friend seemed to act as a sort of conscience for her. "Girl, I know this is none of my business, but you're slipping up, you're being way too obvious. Everyone knows what's going on with you and Óscar. I mean come on now—Óscar, really? What the fuck?" Tati said nothing to her. She just changed the subject or gave her instructions for a new alibi. "What if Teach asks me if you're with me? What the fuck will I say to him?" Tatiana's response was like a punch to the gut. She lashed out at everything. She trashed our history, our commitment to each other, our running into each other at the Greenwich bar, and our friendship. She shot down our dreams. "Fernando's a dickhead." I couldn't stand it anymore. I turned the phone off. I stood up, feeling dizzy, and went into the kitchen. I put her cell phone in the microwave. I set the microwave for five or six minutes and ran out of there. I took refuge in the street, among the panhandlers. When I got back, Tatiana had collected her things. On the fridge was a Post-it with a measly scribble: "I can't talk now. Give me time, give yourself time. Sorry."

Sometimes I would go over to La Sibila. I liked to spend the evenings talking to Macario, but the caretaker's absences were becoming more and more frequent. He had a son with cancer who lived in Valles del Tuy, and he was almost always drunk, waiting for a miracle to happen. His presence was an invitation to robbery, although there was nothing in the house left to steal. It had been looted many times before and there were no valuables left, other than the props from previous productions, covered in mold and cockroach droppings. One night, after Tatiana had left, after sharing a couple of beers with Giménez, I decided to go over to La Sibila to try my luck. It was late, almost midnight. Macario wasn't there. When I opened the door, I heard noises inside the house, feverish laughter and voices singing. My sudden appearance startled them. It was Jacobo and Mimi. They were hiding something. I sensed it from the beginning, but I didn't think anything of it. They were guarding the door to the storeroom where all the junk that could be used as props was stored. Mimi took my hand and led me out to the patio. She offered me a beer. I was pleased to find them there. Giménez wasn't the greatest conversationalist, and the dialectical showdowns between Wong and Ascanio held no attraction for my ailing heart. I needed to find my bearings, ground myself, and for some unaccountable reason, my students helped me to see things in perspective. We sat on the wet wooden flooring of the patio. We made a toast to the end of the world. The beer was warm and bitter. It tasted like tea. Jacobo stayed inside the house, moving things around from one place to another. I didn't ask them what they were doing. I didn't care. "How're you doing, Teach?" Tati's betrayal was common knowledge, an insignificant rumor circulating through the nooks and crannies of Avenida Miguel Ángel, in the breaks in the conflict. Classes had been suspended some days ago for the upcoming municipal elections. The implementation of the Plan República, the military-led operation in charge of setting up and safeguarding polling stations at the schools, would take several weeks to complete. I lied, feigning strength. I deflected the question back to her. I was surprised to see her alone, without her perpetual guardian. "Román's a moron. It's nothing. We fight, but it'll pass. We always fight. Can I ask you something?" "I'm not sure I'll have the answer, Mimi." I put the beer down; it was undrinkable. "Why does love end?" I couldn't help but laugh. It was the first time I had laughed since finding out Tatiana's cell phone password. "No, don't laugh. I'm being serious. You're a know-it-all, you should know the answer." My supposed wisdom was still an enigma to me, but the kids had the impression that I was a kind of guru, that I could offer sound advice for each of their problems. I couldn't come up with a convincing reason. I couldn't say anything. "I love Román. I'm *in* love with Román. I want to spend the rest of my life with Román. Yeah, it may be cheesy, but it's the truth. So does that make me stupid?" "No, Mimi. You're not stupid. You're young, which is similar, but it's not the same thing." "But then why do things change? Why do people stop loving each other?" "Because, with the passage of time, other interests arise. You meet other people, you mature. Life takes you on new paths. There's nothing bad in that. It's all part of growing up." "But I don't want things to change, not for us. I'm not interested in following another path or meeting other people. I want to grow and mature with Román, have children with Román, grow old together." Once, a few months before Lisbon, I had an argument with Tatiana over some nonsense. I didn't want to be at home. I took a stack of tests and went over to La Sibila to grade them. It was night, but not very late. Macario wasn't there. When I entered the house, I heard moans. I couldn't figure out what was going on. I approached cautiously, fearful that a robbery was taking place. In the middle of the room, under the intermittent moonlight slipping in through the window, Mimi and Román were making love. They made love slowly and gently. I didn't dare interrupt that rite of passage. I left without disturbing them. I was touched by their intimacy, their romantic hideaway. In those days, the city was hell. It happened, more or less, around the time when Marcel was arrested, when attacks against protesters became more brutal. My unexpected encounter with the two lovers gave me a breath of peace and hope. I liked knowing that, even though they had sacrificed their youth, they had time to talk about love and to express it to each other, in the midst of the conflict. "What are you laughing at?" "I'm not laughing." I thought carefully about what I wanted to say, choosing my words so as not to disappoint her. "Growing up and maturing alongside another person requires a lot of patience. True love is a bit different than in books or movies. The old age you long for has its attractions, but it's not that romantic. You will have aches and pains and all sorts of crazy habits. If your expectations have not been met by a certain age, your nature may become harsher. Sharing your life with another person, being there, day after day, is more complicated than it seems." "Why?" "Because now you live in your parents' house, you're a student, you don't work, and you spend money you don't earn. I suppose Román is in the same situation." "Román works." "I know, but no one makes a living doing tattoos. It's not enough, Mimi, and even less so in this country." "We're not going to live here. We want to leave." "To go where? The world is no longer what it was. Europe is no longer a destination. The airlines have collapsed. There are no passports. We can't leave." We heard a noise. Something fell inside the house. "What's Jacobo doing?" "Nothing, ignore him. Sometimes he sleeps here. Macario opens the door for him. His dad came home drunk. Not his real dad, the other one, the cop, you know? That kid's life is hell, but he's happy. If half the things that happened to him had happened to me, I wouldn't know how to laugh." She leaned her head on my shoulder and tapped my left foot with her right foot. "So then, I have to assume that my relationship with Román will end; that, in the long run, it will mean nothing, that I'll put him out of my mind and forget him, that I'll meet another asshole and fall in love, that I'll like other things? It's sad, isn't it?" "Not necessarily." "Sometimes I hate you!" She gave me a light, playful hit across the head. "I hate it when you say nothing, when you just give half-assed responses," she said, mimicking me: "'not necessarily,' 'I suppose so,' 'it could be,' 'that's intriguing,' 'that's appealing,' 'that's interesting.' We're not in class. You can be honest with me. Have you stopped loving your wife?" Low blow. My silence showed my discomfort. "Sorry, I didn't mean to say that." "No, it's fine, Mimi. It doesn't matter. I could never stop loving Tati." "And I could never stop loving Román." "You're seventeen years old and I'm turning forty-four." "So okay, then, in twenty-five years, I promise you that Román and I will still be together; moreover, we'll ask you to be the best man at our wedding." "I don't think so. Román hates me." "Don't be dumb. Román doesn't hate you. He admires you." A lot of my colleagues had trouble figuring Mimi and Román out as a couple, because María Victoria was pretty, intelligent, responsible, and disciplined, while Román had the attributes of a bum. He wasn't interested in school. He dropped out in tenth grade without a care and devoted himself to the art of tattooing. He was hateful and hostile toward the teachers. He lacked manners, had no sense of courtesy, and was monosyllabic. My female colleagues thought he was very unsavory because he looked dirty, like he never showered or washed his hair. Román accompanied Mimi to the theater every afternoon and sat motionless during the rehearsals. He was respectful but distant toward me. When we put on *An Enemy of the People,* I asked him to help out with the production, with the technical side of things. At first, he showed some reluctance, but a bit later on he started to feel more comfortable. He even made some valuable suggestions about the lighting effects with flashlights sewn onto the costumes. The conversation drifted in another direction. The closure of the school was inevitable, and there was no money in the budget for a graduation ceremony. The notification that La Sibila had received seemed ominous. We would end up without a school, without a theater, and without a place for ourselves. I vented to Mimi unconsciously, without even realizing it. I told her about feeling tired at work, about the exhaustion of running from one class to another, of having to grade more than four hundred tests filled with meaningless questions. I had lost hope and faith. I didn't feel like working. I felt useless and defeated. "Teach, you can't fall apart. If you fall apart, then we . . ." She made a dropping gesture with her hands, like something crashing to the ground. "Don't say that again. Don't ever feel like that again. Fernando, I'm serious. You're like a god to us." "Look around you, María Victoria. I haven't done anything. I'm nothing but a snake oil salesman, dispensing nonsense. This patio, this house, is my small world. I have nothing else." "Well, it's enough for us. And yeah, so what if you made us out of clay or dog shit or whatever. Regardless, we're here. This theater is the only thing we have. It's our paradise."

Carmelo sprang to mind. Suddenly, in the middle of our talk, I thought of my best friend, the person with whom I'd had the idea of setting up that cultural center. I told her about my sadness at the loneliness of his burial. No one was there. No one attended his funeral. After all those years of teaching, no student had the good grace to go and pay their final respects to him. I sensed the same thing would happen to me the day a stray bullet struck me down in the middle of the highway. Mimi was slow to respond. She seemed to want to say something, but hesitated. She resumed the use of the formal *usted* form with me. "Teach, no . . . You can't compare yourself to Carmelo. Don't do that." Carmelo was my friend and confidant. We graduated together from the same teachers' college, we taught at the same schools (at the Instituto Atenas, at Santo Tomás de Villanueva, at Fray Luis de León), and we were full of ideas for projects. "Believe me, he wasn't like you. If he was alone, if he died alone, it was because he asked for it. I won't say anything else because you're a good person and I know you'd prefer not to know some things." I had already hit rock bottom. Nothing could bring me down further. There was no way back. I gave her a questioning look. "Not everyone is good, Teach." She folded her arms, shivering with cold. "Carmelo was a weird guy. Very weird. He liked to watch us. He paid to watch us." I was stunned and couldn't reply. I didn't know how to. I looked shocked and gasped. "One time, he told Román he'd like to watch us. You know, he'd pay to watch us screw, have sex. And he offered us money, good money. We went to his house and did it two or three times. I didn't like it, but we used the money to go to the movies, to go out and have fun. How else do you think we could afford to eat at the Cine Cittá? We weren't the only ones. He asked several other couples to do it, kids from other years. Teach, did you really not know? Everyone knows that Carmelo was a pervert. He never touched or approached us. He just sat at the back and watched. But he told us things, asked us things. He'd tell us to do this, to do that, to play with this, to play with that. I hated it. It was disgusting. He'd touch himself. He'd cover himself with a sheet and touch himself. The third time we went, he wanted to video us having sex. I told Román I'd rather be broke for the rest of my life than to have to undress in front of that creep again. Then they killed him. Who knows how and why? I'm serious, Teach. Don't compare yourself to Carmelo. I wasn't happy that he died, but I wasn't sorry either. Everyone gets what they deserve. Forget him. You're way better than that prick." She kissed my cheek. It made me uncomfortable (even more so after what she had just told me). I blushed at the gesture. I always suspected that María Victoria was my anonymous romantic pen pal, the one who left me Mario Benedetti poems on the desk after art history classes. Sometimes I would read them with Tatiana, to make fun of my secret admirer's cheesiness. Mimi took my hand and fixed her eyes on the black clouds. "Oh, Teach. Is the world really going to end?"

Jacobo came out to the patio. I wanted to take my hand away from her, but she squeezed it tighter. She noticed my discomfort. Her eyes told me it was okay, that there was nothing wrong in holding hands. Jacobo appeared, invoking curses against the Revolution. He told me he was writing a reggaeton song called "*La ciudad de la sarna*" (The City of Scabs). He shared a few verses: *Todos tenemos sarna / para comprar el champú necesitas el carnet de la patria.* ("We've all got scabs / you need a Homeland card if you wanna buy shampoo.") Mimi made fun of his shaky dance moves and the fact that his lyrics didn't rhyme. The young rapper told me he would have to drop out of school if they closed down Promesas Patrias, because his mom wouldn't have the money to pay for another school. I didn't know what to say to him to make him feel better. I had no convincing arguments. In the Libertador Municipality alone, more than two hundred schools had been closed down. The few that remained open were rundown, with no teachers or budget.

I felt sorry for him. He was a talented boy, with a lot of potential. "What would you have liked to be?" I suddenly asked. I regretted my choice of verb tense, implying that his aspirations would remain unfulfilled. I reframed the question, stressing the present. "Me? A singer, what else! Actually, I don't *want* to be one—I already *am* one. I wanna be like Drake." I had never heard of Drake before. "Teach, don't tell me you don't know who Drake is? Well, I suppose that makes us even then. I don't know who Leonardo da Vinci is and you don't know who Drake is." His tone of voice changed and he burst into laughter. "I'm not gonna be anything, Teach. In this country, a person is nothing. Well, maybe not nothing. A *güevón*—a dumbass. What else? Here we live and die pure dumbasses. And you, Mimi?" he asked, passing the ball and dodging any further questions. "A dumbass like you, my little Jacobo." Laughter. "Although, when I was a kid, I would have liked to be something. Guess!" I remembered her performance in *Richard III*, her ease and confidence, her ability to command the stage. She wasn't a professional actress, but she had the poise, the gestures, the discipline, the will to learn. I hazarded a guess. To my surprise, she said no. She opened her bag. She connected her iPod to a set of speakers. "Don't laugh, okay? And you, keep your mouth shut," she said, pointing at Jacobo. "It's silly, but it's mine, and at one time I dreamed of this." She pressed a few buttons. A light, delicate instrumental piece came on. I forgot everything, about the end of Lisbon, about Tati's betrayal. For a few minutes, my thoughts went blank. "When I was little, my mom enrolled me in ballet classes. I liked it a lot. I still like it. I still watch things on YouTube, but when I started seventh grade the ballet school closed down. The few other ballet academies in Caracas were very expensive."

As she talked, she improvised a few movements, did a few warm-ups and stretches. "I would have liked to continue, but in this country you don't do what you like but what you have to do. This is what I wanted to do, what I always wanted to do, although it's too late for me now." She brought her legs together. She stood on tiptoe, reached out her right arm and closed her eyes. The adagio from Tchaikovsky's *Sleeping Beauty* accompanied her dance on the patio. María Victoria twirled around, began a slow, rhythmic dance, in keeping with the soft and dreamlike melody. She had technique. She knew what she was doing, although she lacked practice. The symmetry between her movements and the orchestral crescendo was perfect, as if the music took her by the shoulders and led her on a walk through the air. There was a harmony of proportions, between her shoulders and her knees, between her concentrated gestures and her tiny feet. I felt sorry for her. I couldn't help thinking that if she had been born somewhere else, at another time, if she had grown up in a less debased environment, she would have been able to demonstrate her talent. I imagined her triumphing on prestigious stages, Lincoln Center in New York, the Palais Garnier in Paris, or a renovated Teresa Carreño Theater in Caracas, earning critical acclaim, receiving praise from prominent dancers, soaring to the heights of fame. She arched her arm over her head and raised one leg. I imagined her being the talk of the town, in the headlines of the cultural pages, and starring in big-budget productions. I had no doubt that if she had had the opportunity, María Victoria would have known how to take advantage of it. But, like many of my students, she was trapped in the cell of our scab-infested city, as Jacobo described it in his epic poem. I knew that she would pass through the world without leaving a trace, condemned to oblivion and the indifference of a jaundiced country, doomed to self-destruction. In the last movement, she dropped gracefully to her knees. "You're amazing," said Jacobo, settling down and curling up in a chair, preparing to sleep outside. I expressed my admiration to her and gave her a hug. I lied and told her that it was possible to succeed, and that if she made the effort, if she worked hard, she could fulfil all her dreams.

It was time to leave. I decided to go home, to my aching loneliness. Before leaving, Mimi came up to me at the door and took my hands. She gave me a big hug. "Teach! I don't want you to be sad. You don't deserve it. Go on, be happy. Do it for us." I don't know how much time we spent holding each other. It was an innocent hug, a sign of genuine affection. Although, maybe if some malicious person had seen us, they might have drawn the wrong conclusions. "Mimi, what's wrong?" Her eyes welled up with tears, threatening to spill over. She wiped them with the sleeve of her sweater. "I'll keep your secret, Fernando. But, please, don't ever say that the only thing in our shitty lives worth living for doesn't make any sense to you. It's not right."

Adagio

THE WALLS OF THE school shook with force. The windowpanes shattered. A high-pitched buzz pierced our eardrums. "The kids! The kids! They're taking the kids!" a woman shouted. I leaned against the doorframe, stunned and deafened. The blast was huge. The PDV gas station in Las Mercedes blew skyward, as part of some sort of sabotage campaign. Those who'd suffered burns jumped into the Guaire River to try to alleviate their pain. When the military arrived, the fighting shifted to Avenida Miguel Ángel. The Baruta Municipality became a barracks to which all the units of the Fort Tiuna Military Base had been transferred. Armored vehicles and water cannons rolled down from the mountain, cutting off access to Las Mercedes and Los Chaguaramos. A cordon of National Guard units, flanked by *colectivos* and SEBIN officers, formed on the overpass.

In the last few weeks we had lived through an unpredictable and anarchic guerrilla war. Complete control of social media did not prevent calls to demonstration. The opposition leaders—forcibly disappeared or imprisoned—were superfluous as well. Discontent, hunger, and humiliation set the agenda. The will to confront the military was no longer a right—it was an impulse, an instinct. Unarmed and starving, with no expectations of victory, the protagonists of the rebellion had decreed war to the death, even though they were aware that they were the weaker side. Protests took place in the neighborhoods of El Paraíso, in Montalbán, downtown, in Santa Monica, in Santa Fe, in Petare, and, with particular fury, on Avenida Miguel Ángel in Colinas de Bello Monte. "They're taking the kids!" the woman shouted again. It was Julia, leaning against the office door, her hair covered with sawdust. The explosion at Las Mercedes was followed by an aftershock. The flare shot up to the overcast sky. The military had no qualms: they attacked the protestors with artillery fire. Within seconds, they destroyed the line of *guarimbas*. Thick clouds of black smoke reached the school. A peppery smell burned my throat, and I couldn't breathe. I went down to Avenida Miguel Ángel, trying to shield myself, paralyzed by agoraphobia, stunned by the crowd running in all directions. I recognized Esteban. He forced my head down and handed me a T-shirt soaked with vinegar. The sounds of gunfire and groans filled the air. Through the shattered windows of the apartments came the anguished shouts of "Motherfuckers! Motherfuckers!" I regained my composure. I managed to drive my demons away, silence the sound of the shotgun. I asked Esteban about the others. I needed to save them, to open the doors at La Sibila where they could hide. The neighbors ran around in disarray. The wind carried away the smoke, leaving the fugitives exposed, making them targets for soldiers who shot at them furiously. At times, the roar of the battle seemed to die down. A tense calm hung over the street that brought a collective sigh of relief. The shooting ceased, until a new attack pushed nerves over the edge. The situation in Chacaíto and Las Mercedes was truly shocking. The dying were piled up in carts, as in medieval times. Ascanio hid a group kids in the stationery store. Giménez and Wong raised their roller shutters to offer shelter to others. In the middle of the street, little Jacobo was banging a drum hanging off his chest, while singing "*La ciudad de la sarna*." He was covered in dirt and someone else's blood, but he kept his huge smile. He kept singing, describing the outrages he had witnessed to the rhythm of reggaeton or bachata, transforming despair into elegy. Jacobo was a child of his time. He had his own Homers and Miltons, his own personal references. His rhymes were encoded with the names of the murderers, the names of the dead, the lost freedom, but also the joy, which he would not renounce. In the midst of the disaster, it was moving to see him marching with his knees high, banging the drum, and speculating on the remote possibility of our victory in his song.

A National Guard patrol car rammed into a utility pole. Four armed guardsmen jumped out, shooting at close range. From nearby windows, debris, parts of washing machines, and refrigerators rained down on them. Gordo Jeanco broke through the guard lines. He went too far. He threw a rock and struck one of the guards' helmets. The other officers ran after him. Jacobo interrupted his drum roll. His face lost its smile. "Jeanco!" the reggaeton singer cried out. They reached him and threw Jeanco to the ground. He scraped his face. "Let go of him! Let go of him!" the students' voices echoed. One of the officers approached Jean Carlo, cocked his pistol, aimed it at his temple, but a blow to his belly prevented him from pulling the trigger. Señora Hernández snuck up out of nowhere like an apparition. She shoved past the officers and formed a shield around Jean Carlo. She stood rooted to the ground, surrounding her son like an impenetrable, protective shell. I read her lips. She was praying. She kept praying, while the guardsmen beat Jean Carlo's legs with the butts of their FAL rifles. They pulled her hair, tried to drag her away, but Señora Hernández didn't cry or move an inch. She was like a stone statue planted into the ground. When the highest-ranking officer kicked her in the back, the angry mob rose up, forcing the officers to run. They took refuge in their vehicle, backing it out fast, running over kids in the street. "Motherfuckers! Sons of bitches! Bastards!" Jacobo resumed his singing, banging the drum again. Señora Hernández collapsed next to Jean Carlo, with broken ribs and a bloody scalp but bolstered by a nervous laugh.

The nightmare wasn't over. Esteban and José Luis appeared on a motorcycle. "Teach, Teach, La Sibila! They're trying to break into La Sibila!" José Luis gave me his seat. I clung to Esteban's back. The protests had never spread so far. Avenida Chama was not normally a place of conflict. When we arrived, there was less noise than on the main avenue. The local residents began to gather around the center. Two SEBIN patrol units were mounted on the sidewalk. I recognized Alexander, leading the raid. At Giménez's bar, they said that Prepucio was the most bitter and unforgiving enemy of the people of Colinas de Bello Monte. He was always there, taking part in the raids and outrages meted out by SENIAT (the revenue service) or SUNDDE (the consumer protection authority), monitoring the residents' strict compliance with the law. I approached with caution. I greeted them, but they ignored me. Although they were armed, the situation was not chaotic. There was a tense calm. Their faces displayed a restless agitation. They banged on the security gate. "No need to break down the door. I have the key." Incensed, Alexander barked orders. I tried to comply, but their blows had destroyed the lock. "There's nothing here, Alexander." "We have intelligence that this center is an arms storage facility." This military terminology was a joke; hateful ministerial jargon. He was right in one way. There was intelligence in the theater, in the arts, but I didn't dare refute him with games of wit. "This place is an arms depot. Don't play with me. Cooperate and I will cooperate with you." The key didn't work. I gave up. He gave the order and they shot the padlock off. They opened the front door. I heard the drum roll, and Jacobo's song in the distance. The crowd gathered around the entrance to La Sibila. There were seven of them and at least fifty of us. Jacobo's appearance reminded me of the recent night when Mimi distracted me by leading me out to the patio. The officers entered. "Alexander! You know I don't lie. I guarantee there's nothing inside this house. You have my word." He stood in front of me, regarding me with extreme suspicion. He was wearing a black uniform and had at least three or four pistols on his body, but something told me he was still the same impressionable kid who hadn't overcome his terror of authority. He bit his lip. "I'm telling you the truth. I swear you won't find anything . . . just some props, paints, costumes. Theater stuff. That's all we do here, theater." Although we were speaking quietly, our conversation echoed. "Please. It's not necessary, really," I insisted. The crackle of his walkie-talkie came to our aid. A broken, disembodied voice, reeling off ridiculous codes, informed him that the conflict in Las Mercedes had escalated and that they required immediate backup. "Let's go." He didn't take his eyes off me. The engines revved. My legs were shaking. I had managed to save them. The kids were still in one piece, still alive, still standing. They had survived another day. Alexander walked over to the waiting patrol car. He opened the door but didn't get in. The drum roll annoyed him. Jacobo circled the car, lifting his knees. He shook his head sideways, with an inexhaustible smile, making up rhymes about the officers' sexuality, their robotic mannerisms, their stupidity, their intellectual poverty, their degeneracy. "Jacobo!" I shouted worriedly. His song turned into the story of a sad man, frustrated by his helplessness and self-conscious about the tiny size of his penis. "Jacobo! Stop it, that's enough!" He turned around and around in circles, banging the drum with joy, accompanying the improvised verses with an ill-fated chorus: "And they called him Prepucio / everyone in the neighborhood called him Prepucio / he was a loser they called Prepucio." "Jacobo, shut your mouth!" I closed my eyes. I heard the pistol go off. Blood splattered my face. There was an utter silence. A few seconds later that seemed an eternity, the mob intervened: "Murderers! Murderers!" My stomach churned. I fell to my knees. The patrol cars took off, chased behind by the local residents who dared to confront them. I didn't want to look. I didn't dare to look, but the kids were desperate, relying on the levelheadedness of my undermined authority. I reluctantly opened my eyes. The body of a child lay in the middle of the street, with a drum resting on his chest. He hadn't let go of the drumsticks. He gripped them tightly, as though they were handlebars. He hadn't lost his smile, despite the hole in the middle of his forehead. Mimi knelt down in front of him. She called out his name, tried to pick him up, but our Jacobo had gone. She kissed him on the head. Then she untied the flag around his waist and wrapped it around her fist. The colors of the flag had darkened. You couldn't see the number of stars for all the blood and dirt. The kids formed a circle around the body. It started to drizzle. Even the sky gave us no respite. Stumbling, I walked into the house, stepping over the wrecked security gate. My heart raced, my asthma and allergies flared up, and I felt like vomiting. The sound of the pistol going off reverberated in my head. It was confused with the other one, with the sound of the shotgun. I opened the storeroom door. I took out the sets, the old props from *An Enemy of the People*. I found the arsenal of artillery: bags of rubble, tin shields, balaclavas, cartridge belts filled with marbles, spiked clubs, slingshots, peashooters, bottles of vinegar, Tupperware containers with cans of Diablito deviled-ham spread—the weaponry of the vanquished rebellion. I looked for the sheet we had used to cover the body of Clarence in *Richard III*. I went back out to the street. Jacobo's head was resting in Mimi's lap. Román had taken the drumsticks out of his hands. I tried to speak to them, but my voice failed me. Little by little, the rain turned into a downpour. Andrea kept vigil, silent and expressionless. The rain running down her neck made the tattooed lizard look as if it was crying. I unfurled the dirty sheet, with yellow stains along the edges. Esteban helped me spread it over the remains of a boy who would never be like the singer named Drake.

• • •

"'No empire justifies breaking a child's doll. No ideal merits the sacrifice of one toy train,'" Moreira recited sadly. He poured me a glass of wine and put something to eat on the table before sitting down. "Don't think for one moment, Fernando, that a humble man like me, of modest intelligence, can polish words to embellish the most atrocious realities. They weren't my words. They were Senhor Pessoa's, who had the strange habit of changing his name and wandering through life with a suitcase full of masks." Jacobo's murder reinforced my self-destructive tendencies. I couldn't get out of bed again. I was paralyzed by a sense of futility, poisoned by emptiness. There was no point in going on or even trying to. I wasn't cold or hungry, even though I had stopped eating for days and the perpetual fog brought icy breezes that froze the room. Principal Monagas put the final nail in my coffin. One afternoon, he left a message on my phone: they would be closing down Promesas Patrias. We wouldn't even get to finish the third term. However, by ministerial decree, the senior year students would be awarded their high school diplomas. The situation was untenable, said the principal. We had no logistic or financial means to keep the school open.

Boredom and listlessness drove me out of the house, leading me to wander the streets like a down-and-out bum. Familiar faces were lined up in front of a broken-down garbage truck. I walked past them, indifferent to their shared humiliation. My neighbors' misfortune barely drew my attention. We had all hit rock bottom. With no expectations, with no emotion, I made my way toward the Centro Polo, meeting the contemptuous stares of the diners at the Cine Cittá. Moreira gave me his condolences. The death of the funny-looking boy who had moved him in *Richard III* kept him awake for several nights. He poured two glasses of wine and opened a tin of olives. "If you don't mind, I will go on with my story, so that you can forget your troubles for a little while. You don't look well, dear friend. You need to get things off your chest, stop wondering what would have happened if this or that had been different. Listen quietly. If you're bored, be patient. I will say it again, there are invisible threads weaving together our fates, and some of the things I went through may help you to regain your lost faith. Despite everything, Fernando, despite what happened in Lisbon, despite those fiends' brutality in killing their own people, I believe in the goodness of God. I am sure that all lived experiences are part of a plan that we cannot understand. Don't lose heart, friend. Come with me to disembark at the Port of La Guaira and to unravel the threads of our parallel lives. Let's make an effort to understand the impossible.

"The trip to Venezuela took two weeks. Agustina stayed silent the whole way there. She refused food and even water. The spectacle of the sea did not move or impress her. Her gaze was lost on the Portuguese horizon, on the world she had left behind. She didn't even know where we were going. That girl was not aware that our spontaneous departure from Lisbon had saved her life. We stopped off in the Canary Islands. With each passing day her silence became amplified. I began to wonder if I had done the right thing. Her sadness just spread like a malignant tumor. The first cracks in my decisions started to show. I realized that I had committed a crime, that I was a criminal. I introduced her as my wife to the port authorities. There was no going back. To escape the punishment of the PIDE we would have to start from scratch in an unknown country called Venezuela.

"Lourenço picked us up in La Guaira. He didn't remember Agustina. When he emigrated, Senhor Urbano's daughter was a little girl, whom he'd completely forgotten. My earliest memories of Venezuela are vague. The language was my first surprise. I didn't understand anything. The people spoke so quickly, with a frenetic and lively rhythm. It didn't resemble the slow Spanish of our Zamoran neighbors.

The Caribbean language was a verbal force that struck me at first as quite abrupt. I was impressed by the mountain, too, this tall peak that reminded me of the landscape of Nogueira. And above all by the heat, the relentless sun that gave us no respite, and which we miss today. All these things went unnoticed by Agustina, because a part of her was still bound up in Lisbon, in solitary confinement in a cell that seemed to be more attractive than freedom in Latin America. My new wife was like a ghost, indifferent to the mesmerizing effect of the modern city, because that Caracas, with its huge highways, with its lights and parties, made Lisbon look like a New Gouvinhas. Next to the things we found here, it seemed as if we had come from a village.

"Lourenço was a man of few words. He never expressed his emotions, in the event he had any. His extreme reclusiveness kept us from fraternizing with other immigrants. We never went to the Portuguese Center or interacted with the people from Madeira. He didn't like Madeirans. He said they were African. For my brother, Portugal ended in the Algarve. He didn't have many friends. He knew how to limit his affections and exist without belonging to a group. From the beginning, he made his conditions clear: 'This is not a place to socialize. No one will give you anything. Work is the only thing that will allow you to get ahead.' Nothing was more odious to him than idle pleasures. He had a bad temper, but deep down he was a good person. Oh how hard it is for me to say 'was' instead of 'is' as we did only just a few short months ago, before the comet struck. What will happen to our correspondence now? Who will send me new books? Lourenço was sick. For years, I had been expecting to receive the news of his death. I was prepared to pick up the phone and hear Teolinda's announcement, but not to face the idea of the end of times. I hope they may somehow have survived, but it's better for my heart to keep speaking of them in the past tense. False hope can be devastating.

"My brother's social defects were compensated for by the kindness of his wife, the good Teolinda." Moreira wiped his eyes. He stayed silent for a few minutes, until he composed himself. The painkiller took effect; his story had captivated me. "The first few years in Caracas were difficult. My relatives' patience was boundless and infinite. Living with another person was not my strong suit. My experience as a husband was not the most fortunate. Lucía's contempt was replaced by my new wife's complete indifference. Agustina did nothing. She didn't know how to do anything. She didn't like the place we lived in, in the Prado de María. At her house in Benfica, she had a room of her own, servants who would cater to her every whim, but now we had to share a cramped boarding room, a bathroom without a door, and a creaking bed. I didn't want to make her feel uncomfortable or treat her with disrespect. I let her have the bed to herself. I got used to sleeping on the concrete floor and washing in the restroom at the grocery store across the street. Lourenço gave me no respite. We arrived in Caracas on a Wednesday, and at noon the next day he put me to work. At first he couldn't pay me, and instead gave me free room and board. He told me if I showed enough commitment my efforts would be rewarded. My brother was a partner in an events company that had just begun to take off. There were no set hours of work. I had no trouble adapting. Ever since I can remember, I have been a servant. Agustina stayed in the house, more dead than alive. Teolinda brought her food, but the trays remained untouched. Eventually, the inevitable happened. Lourenço became annoyed: 'We have a problem.

Here we all have to work, and your wife is a liability.' Teolinda washed, mended, and ironed the neighbors' clothes, and cooked for the other neighborhood residents. She needed help, but I knew Agustina would not be prepared to lower herself. Lourenço threatened to kick us out, to rent the room to other people. He did not like lazy people, like the Venezuelans. My brother said Venezuelan people were lazy and didn't like to do anything, other than get drunk and live life as if it were a party. General Pérez Jiménez was a venerated figure in the Prado de María house. Lourenço's small company was formed during his dictatorship. There was no fixed business plan. One thing led to another. For a time, my brother worked as a waiter in the Salón Venezuela at the Círculo Militar, an exclusive recreational facility for military personnel and their families. There he met other Portuguese northerners, who recognized the commercial potential of organizing managed events. His connections paid off, but everything changed after the events of 1957. People suddenly rose up, dissatisfied with their lot. Outraged by the excesses of the deposed dictatorship, they began to look for scapegoats, and immigrants were the obvious target. The foreigners came to be seen as collaborators of tyranny. A person's word lost all value. People were no longer taken on at face value, because all workplaces had become 'professionalized.' Experience no longer mattered and everything now required a qualification, certification, and meaningless bureaucratic approvals. My brother had to adapt and submit to the rigorous scrutiny that came with democracy, a bombastic concept that no one understood, but that seemed better than the ousted regime.

"Lourenço reminded me of my father. Teolinda saved us from his fury. 'Don't worry,' she said with a smile. 'My husband's bark is bigger than his bite. Leave it in my hands. I promise you things will change. Give the girl time.' But things did not change. Agustina's grief was boundless. Many times, during the early hours of the morning, I heard her weeping and crying until dawn. Teolinda washed our clothes and prepared my meals. She cared genuinely for Agustina, tried to encourage her and bring her out of her voluntary confinement, but her efforts were in vain. My wife had no desire to live and I had nothing to reproach her for. I was to blame for her undoing. I had to take responsibility for her unhappiness. Chance, however, that wonderful strategy that God relies on to carry out His own projects, led me downtown to the Centro Simón Bolívar. I had to open a bank account so Lourenço could pay me my first earnings. I got lost. I had never been to downtown Caracas before. While crisscrossing through the streets, I walked past the shop window of a bookstore. Although I couldn't read, I had always liked books: the smell of the paper, the cover designs, the incomprehensible titles. There was something sacred about words. Moreover, I couldn't forget the fact that the unhappy woman with whom I shared a room in the Prado de María had taught me the alphabet. When I went in, I recognized the Aveiro accent. A man was talking on the phone. I waited, walking up and down the aisles. When he hung up, he asked if he could help me. We recognized each other. We spoke in Portuguese. His name was Sergio Alves Moreira, but his last name had nothing to do with mine. We weren't related, beyond having some remote Moorish ancestor. The bookseller politely asked about me. I told him I was born in Trás-os-Montes, in a hamlet on the outskirts of Gouvinhas. I said I was looking for a gift. Without going into detail, I told him about a relative who hadn't managed to overcome the feeling of saudade. And that's how I met Senhor Torga. The good Sergio went out back in the storage room and returned a few minutes later. He gave me a copy of *Contos da Montanha* (Tales from the Mountain), a grand little book that, in its own way, saved my marriage.

"After that, Agustina changed. Her love of reading, the memory of our land, offered her an opportunity to reinvent herself. She got out of bed, began to eat again, and started treating Teolinda with kindness. When work allowed me to, I would go back to the bookstore in the Centro Simón Bolívar to buy the books recommended by the good Sergio, Portuguese editions brought over as contraband. The second book that I took home was called *A Sibila* (The Sibyl), a beautiful novel written by Senhora Bessa-Luís, with which my Agustina healed herself. Words, Fernando, like medicinal plants, have healing properties. My wife found in the stories of Torga, and in the tragedy of old Quina, Bessa-Luís's protagonist, a haven of peace. Many times, dear friend, the lives of others, even if they are invented, are a mirror that allows us to reflect on our own joys and sorrows. Stories help us to appreciate our good fortune. They open our eyes to the fact that, in the infinite darkness of the universe, we enjoy the privilege of the senses, of awareness, of health, of a beating heart, and that with all these things, it is more than enough to have a good life. The lovely girl from Gouvinhas, the one who taught me my first letters, had bounced back and recovered. She opened the windows of the room, let in the sun. Oh! Will we ever see the sun again? It is difficult to hang on to one's illusions under this perpetual fog. Who would ever have thought that the Caribbean would be shrouded in darkness?

"Agustina gave Caracas a chance. She sailed out the door,

walked down Avenida Nueva Granada, crossing through Los Rosales to Paseo de los Ilustres, and, as if following a treasure map on a desert island, came to the grounds of the Central University of Venezuela. You, a man of the theater, Fernando, will know how to describe the magnetic effect of the stage, of treading the boards, better than I. The advertising posters on the noticeboards around the university led her to the basement of the Aula Magna auditorium, where she met some young people her own age, burning with rebellion and fighting spirit. There was a young man—what was his name? Curiel. Nicolás Curiel, that's it. Lost causes were always Agustina's weakness. Remaking the world was her favorite pastime, so she had no problem in choosing as her first friends this group of angry youths, whose immense arrogance made them believe they knew how to create light or part the water.

"Agustina began to listen to lectures at the university. Her Spanish was better than mine. She had a better ear for it than me, although she was reticent to speak. Our accent was not popular, and after her long period of voluntary confinement she was afraid of being rejected. The 400th anniversary of Caracas was a feast of theater events. During that time, I remember going with her to see a play written by her new friend, young Curiel. It had a biblical name, *The Seven Deadly Sins*. My goodness! How easy it is to play around with what is sacred when you have time to enjoy life! People thought I was her father. I don't know if she was embarrassed by my company, but I liked seeing her smile. Little by little, I realized she had become part of something, and that she wanted to integrate into her new country. Deep down, Agustina was a girl who had had to grow up by force. The illusion, however, was short-lived.

Reality is harsh. Young people can be mean and envious. The art world can be cruel and competitive. Around that time, auditions began for a theater company that would come to be called 'El Nuevo Grupo.' Agustina was excited. She wanted to participate. She made a huge effort to improve her Spanish. She practiced with Teolinda, did the breathing exercises Arlindo had taught her back in Portugal. But, in the end, her audition was a flop. Her accent provoked snorts of laughter. Her nerves failed her and she made a fool of herself, because she forgot parts of her speech and mixed up Spanish and Portuguese. Everything she had achieved in the last few months suddenly fell apart in the face of the destructive sarcasm of the young people. There was this one young fellow, a theater graduate called Cabrujas, who made some nasty comments as I found out later. He invited her to his house on the pretext of offering her a role in a production, of correcting her posture, of training her accent, but all he did was try to woo her with his Venezuelan charm, which was not so well received by foreigners. Agustina hated him. She couldn't stand him. She called him 'the one-eyed man.' You know the saying, right? 'In the land of the blind, the one-eyed man is king.' When Agustina pitted herself against Cabrujas, she lost all chance of gaining a place in the Caracas theater scene, because all the banalities uttered by that loquacious young man were like gospel to his sycophants. Her contempt for him came at a price. All the doors slammed in her face and she earned herself a nickname: the leper. Insecurity destroyed Agustina's talent. She lost interest in the things she loved. Her contempt for Venezuela became her shield. The theater scene was the main target of her gibes and mockery. When she wanted to, Agustina could be very cruel. She mocked the Venezuelan playwrights, who she said had no talent. Often, Fernando, people need to have something or someone to blame for their own misfortunes. It's much easier to go on when you can lay the blame for all your failings at someone else's feet. We admire the truth, but only when it applies to someone else and not when it applies to ourselves. Agustina blamed her misfortunes on Venezuela. She held me responsible for her fate, reproaching me for having chosen this cursed path for her. She never went back to the theater or the university. She never spoke Spanish again or even tried to. She never tried the arepas, the cachapas, or the cheeses from the western region. She never watched television or listened to the radio. Despite Teolinda's kindness, living at my brother's house became more difficult every day. The tension with Lourenço, who kept bemoaning my lack of character, was constant: 'That woman's not even worth the water she washes in,' he said to me many times, unable to understand my sense of responsibility and my commitment to her.

"Reading and the imaginary reconstruction of old Portugal was Agustina's most precious refuge. The Senhores Oliveira, Ferreira, Nemesio, and Cardoso Pires accompanied her solitude and shared her bed. The good Sergio Alves thought the books were for me. Every two weeks, when I passed by the Centro Simón Bolívar, he would comment on the stories and talk to me about the characters as if they were intimate friends. Agustina was a voracious reader. I am not exaggerating when I say that Portugal was alive in those stories, in the flavor of the words that had the taste of our roots. And today, dear Fernando, despite the fact that our country has been destroyed, I dare say that it remains intact. As long as Senhor Torga's books exist, there will be riches to explore in Trás-os-Montes and a sandy path that leads to

Gouvinhas. Writers are well versed in the science of time travel and know better than anyone how to make dewy-eyed readers take a trip back into their childhood.

"Agustina lost her vitality. She rotted from the inside out, eaten away by bitterness, despair, loneliness, and the painful memory of Arlindo, whom she never forgot, and whose name she called out at night, hugging her pillow. Many times, I feared losing her. I imagined coming home and finding the room empty. But she had nowhere to go. She had no friends in Caracas or money. She had no identity, because for legal purposes, as if it were a heteronym created by Senhor Pessoa, her real name was Lucía. I got used to living with a ghost, with a woman I never touched, and with whom I didn't know how to communicate. I had the false impression that I had saved her life, but in reality, our marriage was a life sentence for her.

"It happened during lunch one day. Teolinda was making a *caldeirada*, a fish stew. Lourenço read the news aloud: the Estado Novo had fallen. Prime Minister Marcelo Caetano had been removed from office. Portugal was free. The Carnation Revolution had triumphed and the PIDE barracks had been overrun by joyous crowds. My brother sat silent. Teolinda cried discreetly, with quiet but uncontainable emotion. There was no conversation at the table. We had nothing to say to one another, because for us Portugal was Salazar. There was no other way to understand it. He had been dead for four years, but he kept pulling the strings and watching over us with his shadow. I went back to the bedroom. Agustina was lying in bed, reading a novel by Vergílio Ferreira. I told her what had happened. She didn't react. She continued reading, annoyed by my interruption. But that night, she lay down on the floor and patted my shoulder. She woke me up. 'Moreira. I want to thank you for all you have done for me, but you know I don't belong here. Please allow me to return to Portugal.' It's late, Fernando. You should go home. Take care of yourself. Another day I will tell you the rest of the story."

• • •

I hit a dead end trying to find Tatiana. Yolanda blocked my phone number. My in-laws' indifference made it clear whose side they were on. Tatiana and I hadn't spoken to each other since the day she left. When they killed Jacobo, she finally sent me an email. She wanted to say how sorry she was about what had happened. Jacobo's murder was the best excuse she found to venture an explanation for her infidelity. I wanted to forgive her. If she came back, we could start over again, even though the details of her betrayal were burned into my memory. I refused to accept defeat, much less without an argument to help me understand the reasons for her estrangement. The WhatsApp texts kept hitting me like a punch to the gut. They wouldn't stop coming at me. They insisted on ripping me apart. She had asked him to take her to the limit, to bite her swollen nipples, like the time they made love in the Montaña Suites or when they met up in Santa Inés, in Yolanda's apartment. That creep, with lousy spelling, kept repeating how much he'd enjoyed penetrating her and, with puzzling cheesiness, promised her he would be by her side forever. The evocation of their encounters was explicit. They described everything, destroying my sanity with every mention of their erotic stunts. "If I'm not speaking to you, it's because I don't know what to say, because I don't know how to justify what happened, because if you read what I think you read the day you put my cell phone in the microwave, then, I have no defense." Her coldness was more offensive than her discretion. All our history reduced to an email. The destruction of our world summed up in a pathetic email. Mutual understanding between us had disappeared. She had another vocabulary, another dialect, as if she was talking to a stranger or a customer at work. Her confession seemed rehearsed, a performance. "I guess all we can do now is make the separation formal. There's no point discussing divorce, because neither of us is in a position to afford it." I read the email over and over, sitting on the living room floor, naked, with the laptop resting on my knees, lost between the glimmer of the past and the bitterness of her defense, because in her accusation, in her testimony about our failed relationship, she said that many of the things that happened had happened because of me. "I became invisible to you. You had eyes only for your damn theater. And when I fell apart, when I broke down, you weren't by my side. You left me when I needed you the most. And the worst thing is, you didn't even realize that I was crying out for you." Heartbroken, soul destroyed, I tried to grasp time with my hands, to repair the cracks, to reverse the breakup, to be more attentive. One by one, the accusations metastasized. ". . . because, like a fool, I had sacrificed everything for you. And what did you give me in return, Fernando? When I wanted to have a child, you told me the best thing to do was wait, because you were counting on things improving in the short term in this shithole of a country. When I wanted to move to Lima with my sister, with jobs lined up for the both of us, when it was still possible to leave, your aunt had her stroke. And even though you knew her situation was irreversible, you chose to stay and watch over her, waiting for a miracle. I don't know how many years have passed, but

Rosaura is still lying there like death warmed over, serving as an excuse for your mother to manipulate you, to take away what little you have left, to compete with me and to defeat me. Your mom beat me, I accept it. But she beat you, too." Memories rushed in. I didn't see it coming. She never hinted at her despair. She never said, "I need you." "You always cared more about your kids at the theater group than what was happening at home. While I felt the need to be loved, to feel that someone cared, to feel alive, you were hell-bent on running a mediocre theater group, confusing Colinas de Bello Monte with Broadway, with seven or eight assholes who will forget about you as soon as they graduate from high school, as has been happening for the last twenty years." The memories of our encounter at the Greenwich bar kept me awake at night. We got wet in the rain walking back to my apartment. We saw each other naked. We made a commitment. Despite my complete lack of rhythm, we danced salsa. Tati liked salsa erótica. With her I discovered a raunchy and melodic universe. We did our chores to the sounds of Tito Rojas and Grupo Niche. We cleaned the house while listening to tawdry songs about sordid romances in sleazy motels. She danced alone, hugging the vacuum cleaner. I liked to tease her, to sing in her ear, exaggerating the suggestive lyrics. I even learned them by heart from listening to them so much: *Aquí estamos tú y yo / con los labios hinchados / de tanto besar y besar de tanto haber amado / aquí estamos tú y yo / empapados en sudor / y regresando de la fantasía que produce hacer el amor*. ("Here we are, you and me / with our lips bursting / from so much kissing and so much loving / here we are, you and me / dripping sweat / and coming down from a fantasy of love-making.") I acted like a hood, and she liked it. She liked me to sing to her at night, too, to help her get to sleep. She found it hard to fall asleep, so I would lull her with disjointed lyrics. Tears welled up in my eyes and broke my reverie. On the day of our civil marriage, backed by a rock band composed of ex-students, I took a gamble with my wedding gift to her. *Sólo Bolero* by Gilberto Santa Rosa was one of her favorite CDs. She kept a copy of it in the car and on her iPod. She played it whenever she was cooking or taking a shower or studying. My former students had done the arrangement, and after the wedding toast, I stepped up to the mike and sang her a song from the CD. It was a small, discreet ceremony. Carmelo and Yolanda were our wedding attendants. The song was hard to sing, with long lyrics, but I knew she would like it because it talked about us. As I replayed the scene in my mind, I searched for it on YouTube. It took ten minutes to load. The government's website blocking strategy was a farce, a dumb stunt to recruit desperate cybernauts and increase the number of members of the United Socialist Party of Venezuela. The idea that only Homeland cardholders would have access to the internet was a botched threat. Ten minutes after Conatel decreed that the state would have all control over internet use, peddlers sold pirate access codes on the highway. I banged my fists against my temples. I clicked play on the YouTube video: *Hablan de un amor alucinante / tan intenso y fascinante / como el sol de primavera*. ("They talk about a mind-blowing love / as intense and enchanting / as the spring sun.") The person who uploaded the song had added GIFs of elves and anime dolls to the video as a form of sugarcoating. I squeezed my tear-filled eyes closed. Each verse was a blunt reminder of how she had given herself to Óscar, of the dirty words they said to each other, of the virtual sex they engaged in, while we were still sharing the same bed. *Cuentan de un amor que es tan perfecto / tan hermoso y tan honesto / que se exhibe donde quiera.* ("They tell of a love that is so perfect / so beautiful and sincere / a love that has no shame.") Tatiana, in her white wedding dress, looked at me from the table, leaning on her elbows with a glass of champagne in her hand. She was happy and emotional. In spite of everything we'd lost, I knew I hadn't imagined her happiness. What we experienced together was real. We had something true and genuine. But the image of her with her lover broke the spell. The words in her WhatsApp message burned in my brain: "Suck my tits. I want you to cum on my tits." I threw the laptop against the wall and ran down the hall to the bathroom. I turned on the hot, brown water and stood under the shower. The boiler blew. My back was red and icy from the cold. I stared out the window and felt weighed down by the ominous horizon, covered in dark clouds portending the end of the world. "I'm responsible for what happened, Fernando. There are no excuses to justify it and I'm sorry you found out the way you did. I would have preferred to spare you that pain, that unpleasantness. I don't feel good about hurting you. I want you to be well and I want you to be happy. With me, clearly, you weren't. But I think the time has come for us to go our separate ways. When was the last time we spoke? When was the last time we made love? Why continue living like this, together yet apart, in the same bed but in such different places? Right now, I have only one conviction: to leave this fucked-up country. I can't stay here. I can't, Fernando, I really can't. You can wear your rose-colored glasses all you want. Things won't change. I hope your students can make you happy. I couldn't. It's true, I would like to be able to face you, to tell you all this looking you in the eye. It's the least I could do, but I can't. I don't know how to. It hasn't been easy for me. I made sacrifices, too. I lost, too. Give me time, give yourself time." The landline rang and shook me out of my torpor. It rang long and shrilly. I fantasized it was Tati, calling to tell me it was all a mistake, that she'd be here soon, that we'd order a pizza and watch TV together. I picked up the receiver anxiously. The disappointment was immediate: it was my mom. She needed money.

I had promised I would never visit her again, but I knew how weak my promises were. While Rosaura was still ill and incapacitated, keeping my distance would be negotiable. My mom never liked Tati. She said she was spoiled and stuck-up and that she looked like a whore, and that one day our difference in age would be our undoing. I hadn't been back to La Candelaria in a long time. Colinas de Bello Monte had become my perfect bubble, a cesspool in which I managed to keep my head above the muck. The downtown area was an abyss, a strange place where the inhabitants spoke a different language. The Candelaria of my childhood, full of noise and color, had disappeared. The area had become gray, polluted, and dangerous. All the businesses had their roller shutters down, turning the main square into a stronghold for beggars and the inflated corpses of dogs. The apartment building was rundown and permeated by the smell of bleach. At night, drunks used the entrance as a urinal, and the neighbors had agreed to take turns in cleaning up the mess every morning. A few months back, during the last round of protests, the janitor's office had burned down. The janitor had been branded a "patriotic informant" by the mob. A group of rebels threw flaming cardboard through his half-open window. The poor wretch burned to death, because the protesters had put a chain around the security gate. The elevator didn't work.

It was an open hole in which sewage accumulated. Despite the rampant misery, my mom was still dressed in red, deeply committed to the ideals of the Revolution.

Aunt Rosaura was wasting away in bed, in an absurd fight against time, demanding attention we couldn't afford to give her. Her terminal illness allowed my mom to exploit and manipulate others at will. I entered the apartment without greeting her and went straight to the bedroom. Rosaura, the once robust and energetic Rosaura, had become gaunt and withered. I shooed the mosquitoes away from her face. "That girl cheated on you. I warned you she would," a voice full of sarcasm and laughter called out from the hallway. "What do you want?" I asked, annoyed. The photo of the Eternal Commander, surrounded by Afro-Latin saints and pictures of the Virgin Mary, stared at me from the nightstand. Memories of our last argument came flooding back to me (random words, insults, tears of rage). It occurred the year before, during one of the many rigged elections. A neighbor called to tell me what had happened. Despite the fact that the government had complete control of the area, they called snap municipal elections. Opposition groups had somehow managed to organize themselves, with little but no real chance of victory. Even so, the incumbents said, if more people were to join the fledgling opposition movement, they would have to find more cunning strategies to stymie people's discontent. Since 1998, my mom had always been first in line at the Chimborazo High School to cast her vote for the advancement of socialism. As remote as the chance was that the government would lose in the municipal elections, she came up with a Machiavellian plan to ensure their success. The neighbor told me that my aunt Rosaura, who wasn't able to feed herself or go to the bathroom alone, had somehow managed to go and vote in a wheelchair. Under the "assisted voting scheme," an army guy guided her hand and enabled her vote to be cast for the Revolution. When I visited her, my aunt's fingers were withered and covered in purple ink. The argument with my mom was heated and intense. I'd never spoken to her like that before. That was the last time we talked. Her request for money offended me. I could no longer restrain myself. I told her I wouldn't give her anymore money and that she should stop counting on me to support her excessive spending habits. "You'll be back. You always come back. You're weak. Get it off your chest if it makes you happy, but, sooner or later, you'll be back. Don't drag up all that stuff about your aunt again. She wanted to go vote and I took her. End of story. I don't see what the problem is." I felt like punching her in the face, knocking her teeth down her throat. We didn't have much to say to each other. I didn't want to be there. She came straight to the point, asking for money for some medicine. I told her the truth: I had none to give her. I had no money or work. I kissed Rosaura on the forehead, between the scabs and the larvae, with the feeling I would never see her again. I regretted not being able to do anything for her, resigned to her fading away.

My mom tried to demean me by throwing in my face the fact that Tati had abandoned me. She doubted my masculinity and openly questioned the number of lovers I'd had to share Tati with. She said it was natural that I would be deceived, because it was evident I couldn't satisfy her in any way. I was immune to her scorn. Her contempt was the same as always. My conception was an accident, the result of an inopportune infatuation that turned into disappointment. My existence was a reminder of a wound, of deep heartbreak.

If not for my aunt, I would have ended up in a shelter or, with any luck, abandoned in a cardboard box beside a trash can or utility pole. Rosaura was a primary school teacher. When I was a child, I used to go with her to the classes she taught in the neighborhood. She was upright and strict, but kind and loving, too. Our good humor vanished as soon as we returned to the house and were faced with my mom's downcast mood. It wasn't easy to make her laugh or get her to play board games with us. One time, when I had grown up, Rosaura explained the reason for my mom's discontent. She told me about my dad, a specter I barely remembered, a foreign accent, a metallic click, the blast of a shotgun. "I don't have any money. Goodbye. Don't call me again. If anything happens to Rosaura, I have other ways of finding out about it." I went downstairs. Time folded back on itself and I was an impressionable child again. My dad was the smell of a brown leather jacket, an occasional visitor who would sometimes pat me on the shoulder or on the back. I heard the shot. There was a lot of noise. The street was in uproar. It was 1989 and the frenzied mob was looting and ransacking the businesses on the block. Caracas was on fire. The man in the brown leather jacket had spent the night in our house. When it happened, my mom hadn't come home from work yet. I heard the blast. I opened the door. The shotgun was on the ground. The wall was splattered with a trail of blood and pieces of skull. I screamed desperately. I ran out into the street, pursued by the image of a monster. People around me were running helter-skelter, making off with household appliances and sides of beef over their shoulders. Angry men and women lugged televisions and refrigerators. I let myself be carried along by the stampede, trying to hide in the midst of the commotion. I started running aimlessly, with a juice blender I picked up from the ground, fleeing the pursuit of the headless ghost. Since that day, I developed an absolute terror of crowds. They intimidate me and make me feel dizzy. My throat constricts and I lose all sense of balance. Tatiana never understood my inability to attend protest marches. She thought my agoraphobia was nonsense, an excuse with which to justify my incorrigible cowardice. I lost her because of my weaknesses. If I'd had the courage to go to the marches with her, to demonstrate alongside her, to cross the Guaire River with thousands of people being pursued by the National Guard, her feelings for me would not have changed.

I returned to Colinas de Bello Monte in a *carrito por puesto,* a passenger car that operates as a bus service. Some young people got on at Plaza Venezuela. They said they were media and communications students. They were carrying a cardboard television and improvising a mock newscast called El Bus TV. The passengers put aside their apathy for a few minutes and paid attention to them. The unemployed journalists spoke about Lisbon. The death toll was untold and rising. The center of Portugal was a burning blaze that hadn't gone out. The migration crisis was wreaking havoc in Spain, France, and Morocco. A plague had erupted. Epidemics and viruses were beginning to appear. The heatwave in Europe was causing unprecedented ecological crises. The Caribbean sky, by some strange butterfly effect, was still hidden under a dense, immovable mass of black clouds that had caused airplane accidents. Maiquetía's air traffic controllers had gone on strike indefinitely. They didn't want to lose any planes. The young people from El Bus TV also spoke about a photo that had gone viral, an image that had circulated uncensored on social media for a few days. It was an image of the famous Lisbon sculpture, the Padrão dos Descobrimentos or Monument to the Discoveries, located in Belém, on the north bank of the Tagus River. This landmark, built in memory of Henry the Navigator, ended up lodged into the side of a mountain in Sintra still looking pristine and intact. The stone mass had been lifted from its location at the port and had been hurled more than twenty miles through the air, where it found a new home, becoming the most emblematic memento of the tragedy. A group of Red Cross relief workers had taken the photo, which turned into a meme.

I entered the bar and ordered a bottle of gin. Ascanio and Wong were recounting the glory days of the neighborhood, back when it was still possible to have fun and the residents of Colinas de Bello Monte spent their leisure time together. Giménez was proud of the photographs hanging on the wall in his bar. The images showed scenes from the first (and only) inter-neighborhood softball tournament that was played on the old Lagoven Petroleum site in Los Chaguaramos, now a kindergarten at the Bolivarian University. Team Giménez-La Buhardilla (when it was still a Spanish tavern) won first place in the contest, prevailing over the vast group of Chinese restaurants, the Forchettone, La Cuevita del Este, and the most seasoned rival, the Central Madeirense supermarket. The brass medals hung rusting in the trophy cabinet. Ascanio claimed the event had taken place in such and such a year. Wong disagreed. I filled my glass up with gin and downed it without taking a breath. On the table at the back of the bar, next to the restrooms, I recognized Macario's shabby profile. He was sitting alone, in front of a glass of anisette. I went over to say hello. He didn't want to look at me. He barely responded to my gesture. When I turned to walk off, he called out my name. He stammered. "I-I . . ." He struggled to go on, his bad conscience eating him up inside. "It . . . It was me who betrayed the boy, Teacher. I told SEBIN about the weapons. If they went to search the house, it was because I turned them in." At the bar, Ascanio was describing the strategy they'd used to make the last out and win the softball tournament. I couldn't reply. I had nothing to say. "You know that my son is sick. They offered me some medicine, a treatment. I'm still waiting for it. I knew that Jacobo and the other girl, the chubby one, were stashing away some unusual things in the storeroom, Molotov cocktails, gasoline, and rocks. When SEBIN came looking for me, I had no choice but to tell the truth. But I didn't want them to kill him like a dog. He was a nice kid." Silence. Contempt. Pity. "It was you they wanted, Teacher. SEBIN came to La Sibila looking for something they could use against you, but I had nothing to give them. All I knew was that the kids were using the storeroom as an arms depot. I gave them up, it's true, but the officer who killed him wasn't really after them. It was you he wanted." I had the urge to take the glass out of his hand and smash it over his head. I walked away without saying a word. I sat down at the bar. The banality of the conversation about an old softball game was more appealing than the confession of a miserable old wretch. I needed to drink until I passed out, until I disappeared. I downed a glass of gin in a single gulp. And then I downed another. My palpable sense of unease, my determined efforts at self-destruction, interrupted the bland debate. "Hey, Teacher, are you alright there, is everything okay?" asked Wong. Tati kissed me again, fondled me, asked me to sing her a song because she couldn't fall asleep, and then turned aside to write a message on WhatsApp: "Meet me later. Don't worry, I'll be with Yolanda. Ha, ha, ha. Don't worry. He won't find out. The only thing that matters to him are his kids from La Sibila. Don't be late. I miss your hot salty taste." Happy emoji with tongue out.

Requiem

THE TABLES WERE LAID with snacks. The kids were sitting on the floor, their clothes all rumpled. My arrival silenced them. Gordo Jeanco led off a rowdy applause that was accompanied by cheers and hurrahs. Giménez gave me a resigned shrug, pointing at the organizers of the ceremony with his chin. Wong had served up a feast on the bar counter: pots of fried rice and chop suey. A beaming Ascanio was garnishing the other dishes. The glass doors of the trophy cabinet were wide open. The brass medals from the Colinas de Bello Monte inter-neighborhood softball tournament had been laid out on the dessert cart.

My headache suddenly stopped. I replayed the last few hours in my mind and felt ashamed. I cracked up and went to pieces. My nerves and my will were shattered. Alcohol just fueled my distress. Giménez told me if I wanted to kill myself I should do it somewhere else and not in his bar. I had good reasons to fall apart: hunger; Tatiana's leaving me; Macario's betrayal; my aunt's illness; my mom's stupidity; Jacobo's death. And in the background, Lisbon, the humanitarian crisis in Europe, plus the images that had begun to secretly circulate: the ring of fire photographed from the hilltop town of Elvas; the highways of Extremadura flooded with people on foot, trudging along, their arms sagging from the weight of the children they were carrying. I told my barroom buddies about the situation in the schools. There would be no graduation ceremony for the senior class at Promesas Patrias this year because of budget constraints. As for the other high schools in the municipality, a decree had been issued by the Mayor's Office of Baruta, one of those governmental authorities that operated in the services of the Revolution after elections had been rigged. It decreed that certificates and medals would be handed out at a single event to be held at the Concha Acústica amphitheater, with a speech by the governor, tributes to the founders of the nation, and various other kinds of patriotic shit. Ascanio and Wong were the main witnesses of my defeat. I shared with them my sorrows and regrets, and how bad I felt about the kids' misfortune. They accompanied me home under a cold night sky. I woke up at noon, paralyzed with grief. The smell of food overwhelmed my instincts. Like a wild animal, I scarfed down the plate of rice that was on the table. I ate with my hands, staining them with soy sauce. I couldn't remember the last time I had eaten a hot meal. There was water; brown, but liquid. I had enough time to take a shower and to fill up a few buckets and pots to wash the dishes in. My only suit, a little moth-eaten and musty smelling, was spread out on the sofa in the living room. Next to it, a note written on a napkin: "Dear Teacher, have a good rest. We'd like you to come to Giménez's bar tonight. We want to do something for you and the kids, a little something that we know you will like. Ascanio & Wong."

Ascanio called for silence. He pretended to be standing at a lectern. Hamming it up, he welcomed everyone to the end of school event. Laughter at the kids' table. They sat me in the front row, with the chairs lined up facing the bar. Señora Hernández, with a bandage on her arm, stood at the back watching us. Our master of ceremonies announced the program for the evening. The ceremony began with a minute of silence in honor of fallen classmates. We stood up. Leonidas said an Our Father. Esteban took my right hand, Mimi my left. The others completed the circle. It was a calm and solemn moment. With my eyes closed, I recalled the faces of all the students killed during the lost battles. But instead of lamenting their misfortune, of submerging myself in the pain of their premature passing, I managed to visualize them happy and carefree together, running after a ball through the Plaza Alfredo Sadel, commenting on the latest Marvel movie, or feigning attention in a boring art class, trying to stay awake, supporting their chins with their hands so their heads wouldn't fall on the desk. I liked to think they were still alive and that somehow they would continue to grow, in a place where we couldn't see them. The minute of silence was like a hallucinogenic drug that united us. The smell of the spring rolls carried us to an artificial paradise—devastated and barren, but ours.

Wong broke the ice: "A few words from our graduate, Jean Carlo Hernández." Gordo approached the pretend lectern with a few crumpled, handwritten notes in his hand. His initial laughter was contagious: "Distinguished Señor Giménez; honourable Wong; dear Señor Ascanio, co-creator of this parody; our Favorite Teacher, Fernando; family and friends." He interrupted his warm welcome. His expression changed. He had a frog in his throat. He reviewed his notes, looking somewhat embarrassed. "I tried to write down a few words this afternoon, but I don't think they make much sense. I'll share them with you and maybe together we can find the meaning." He started reading. His legs were shaking. He didn't finish his first sentence. He took a deep breath and then exhaled slowly, like we did in rehearsals at La Sibila. He gathered his confidence and stood up straight. "I'd known Jacobo Sánchez ever since he was a little kid. He was as full of life as he was a pain in the ass. He liked to play with older kids. He wasn't comfortable around kids his own age. He was always drawing attention to himself, rapping about his daily routine, singing about the shortage of products in the cafeteria, echoing the catcalls of the guys calling out to girls on the street, or cursing the outrages committed by the National Guard. He never shut up. I often thought of him as a nuisance. We all knew him. He was our friend. Jacobo was killed for being young, for exercising a nonexistent right in a country where dreaming is a crime. They killed him for playing a drum on the street. Today we miss him." He paused, until he composed himself. "I met Marcel Hidalgo in second grade, when my family moved to Caracas. He didn't like to go unnoticed either. But he had his own way of attracting attention, because Marcel speaks better than all of us put together. He writes well, too, without any spelling or grammar mistakes, the kind that make our teacher Fernando's hair stand on end. Marcel wants to study Political Science, despite the fact that the universities are closed and that everyone tells him the Central University's Faculty of Economics and Social Sciences is a rat hole. Marcel's a smart guy, who reads a lot and knows what he's talking about. He doesn't talk shit like we do. Everyone knows him. He's our friend. He's my best friend. Marcel is imprisoned in La Tumba. People say the last time he was beaten up in there, they pulled out his teeth. Marcel was jailed for standing his ground, for saying no. He gave his freedom for this shitty country, to which we owe nothing, but for which we ourselves are willing to die. Today we miss him, just as we miss many of our friends, kids I never knew, but those I saw many times in the marches. Kids who ran alongside me, breathing in tear gas, their only hope being to see another day, whatever it brings. Juan Pablo Pernalete, Armando Cañizales, Neomar Lander, Miguel Castillo, and many others. I was there. I saw them fall. It could happen to anyone. I wonder who was saved: was it them or us, who are still here? To make things worse, from one moment to the next, the world is threatening to end. What happened to Lisbon put us on notice. And we're supposed to give thanks to God for keeping us safe." Although his hands were trembling, he read slowly, his voice steady. The group listened attentively.

"I don't want to thank God for anything. I don't want to play along with that jerk." He looked up toward the sky. "But I don't want to feel sorry for myself either. I'm tired of feeling we have to be grateful for this shitty life we're living. If God is responsible for so much grief, for the daily horror, for the murder of our friends, then I'm not interested in his mercy, much less his overrated paradise. I don't want to meet him. I refuse. We're alone, that's the only truth. We're not going anywhere. We have no past or future and our present is an insult. We don't even have sunshine. The cold is here to stay, along with the acid rain that irritates our eyes and reminds us that the officers can come and kill us whenever they like. Our generation suffers from the 'Lisbon syndrome,' knowing that the things we love are finite, knowing that there is no tomorrow, knowing that we won't have enough time to do anything worthwhile, that we will disappear without leaving any kind of mark, because we don't matter to anyone, because our existence has no relevance. We have no horizons. We have no dreams, they're forbidden. The only thing we have, the only thing we can boast of, is our friendship. And, in the midst of this shit, this rage—" his voice broke "—in the midst of this lost time, friendship is what I want to celebrate tonight, together with the best people I know. Tomorrow or the day after tomorrow it will all be over. We will be shot dead at point-blank range, and if we're lucky, if we can save ourselves from the bullets, then some asteroid will get knocked out of orbit and finish us off that way. There won't even be time to ask ourselves if it was worth it. The truth is, there's not much to save. We were only happy at La Sibila, where we played at putting on serious dramas, with political metaphors that were unintelligible to the majority of the audience, and under the supervision of a stubborn fool who insisted on repeating to us that we had to believe in ourselves and that life was worth living. We tried, Teach. We really did." He put the paper in his pocket and returned to his seat. Mimi gave him a fist bump. Andrea followed suit. Esteban and José Luis did the same. Señora Hernández had tears in her eyes. Ascanio broke the peace, applauding loudly, calling out "Bravo!" Then, with his irritating enthusiasm, he said one shouldn't be so pessimistic, and he repeated the motto that, sooner or later, we would all go out onto the street and shout for our freedom.

"A few words from the Favorite Teacher, Fernando Morales." Wong gave me his place. I stood up awkwardly, tripping over a tray of ribs. When I left the apartment, I hadn't considered the idea of giving a speech. I had no idea what I could say, much less after hearing Jean Carlo's fatalistic admission. The kids looked at me with expectation in their eyes, hoping I'd offer them something palpable, something plausible. But I was conflicted, because I thought Gordo was right. I knew, however, that I couldn't let them down. Their hopes had nothing to do with my defeated will, but with my responsibility as a teacher. I knew I wouldn't have another chance to make an impression on them. I suspected this would be my last class. One by one, I looked them in the face. The words came effortlessly. "I've lost count how many times over the years I've been chosen the Favorite Teacher of a class, but this recognition is always a thrill for me, a gesture of affection for which I feel great satisfaction and pride. I usually prepare a few words of thanks. I work on a short speech a few weeks ahead of time, which I then read at the ceremony, peppering it with quotes and pausing for effect to make me sound like a brilliant man. Many of those speeches are filled with pompous phrases and sappy lies about freedom and sacrifice. For years, I've been telling my students that they have the world at their feet, and that if they do their part they will get what they want; that you will fulfil your dreams just because you have them. But I can't lie to you. You don't deserve such hypocrisy. It isn't fair to persist in this deceit. But I don't want to discourage you either, because, perhaps without realizing it, you more than any other class have shown me the value of courage and persistence. I've watched you grow, mature, stumble, and get back up on your feet again. I don't know of any other generation that's had to live through such adverse circumstances. Many times I said to myself: If the kids had had better opportunities, I don't doubt they would have made the most of them. No goal would have been impossible for them. However, after all we've lived through, I realize my lie. And though you may find it difficult to appreciate, and as hurtful as it is, this hostile and humiliating reality is what has brought out the best in each of you, what has made you what you are today. Who knows, maybe if we had everything at our fingertips, if everyday life was less of a struggle, we would miss what is essential, and it would take us a long time to discover what matters most, something you've had to learn by force, with a maturity inappropriate for your age, and while having to face a ruthless enemy that has betrayed and murdered your childhood and robbed you of the beauty of adolescence.

"For a long time, our life has been hell. We got used to thinking with our stomachs. You have been hungry, you have witnessed families being torn apart, you have watched your friends die, murdered in cold blood. You have also realized that, day after day, they are taking away your future, whatever future there is. To top it all off, the world is threatening to blow itself up completely. Not only have we lost hope, but an incurable virus and a stray asteroid have come along to remind us of our worthlessness. It may seem like a consolation or a pep talk, but amid this scenario of utter desolation, I can only express my admiration and respect. What you have done is heroic. You may not have had the best formal education. I'm aware that your oral and written expression skills are not the greatest. Some, it's true, can't distinguish accented from unaccented words, and others confuse Rómulo Gallegos with Rómulo Betancourt." Gordo Jeanco, laughing and embarrassed, looked down at the floor. "I don't doubt that our classroom work could have been better, but what you have experienced in this time, the way you have endured loss and pain, is a very valuable life lesson for which there are no exemplary courses or theories. Learning how to function as a member of society has been a harrowing experience. But you haven't wasted your time, kids. Every second lived in this no man's land is an unforgettable lesson. And when those clouds part, when we see the sun again, because I swear that one day the sky will open up again, it will help make you better people, good and decent men and women, whose steps will always be true." Something caught my eye: Román's hand was resting on Mimi's belly, as if cradling it. "I wish I had enough conviction to tell you that you will rediscover your dreams, that happiness is within reach, that the future will be full of opportunities for you, but I'm not sure this can happen. It would be irresponsible of me to say so. If it were up to me, I would have given you the world, but I am just a high school teacher who tried, who did what he could to provide you with a few tools with which to go out into the world, and at the same time I know that my efforts have not been enough. If I have failed you, then I am sorry. I too am afraid. I too am tired and exhausted. If I've managed to stay on my feet it's only because you have prevented me from collapsing in a heap. I ask you, please, no matter what happens, don't lose faith. Don't give in, don't throw in the towel. I disagree with you, my dear Jeanco. I don't accept your feeling of resignation. You have your whole lives ahead of you. True, they may be short-lived, but they're lives that can make a difference. Even though it's forbidden to dream, I say—dream. I will take responsibility for saying this. We are still standing. We don't know for how long, but we're here. And we are worth something, even if our adversaries try to convince us that we are worth nothing. Thank you, kids. From the bottom of my heart. Believe me, what I have been able to do for you is nothing compared to everything you have done for me."

Ascanio's lack of reserve broke the solemn mood. He was the only one who applauded. The students were staring blankly at the closed windows or the stains on the terracotta tiled floor. Wong approached the bar. He had the names of each of the graduating students written down on a napkin. Giménez stood behind the dessert cart and, one by one, passed the brass medals to Wong. Antonio read out the names slowly: "José Luis Álvarez." A beaming smile. I took the medal out of the MC's hands. José Luis leaned forward. "Teach! Thank you." "And to you." "Andrea Echenausi." She approached the pretend rostrum blank-faced. She bowed mechanically and stepped back without taking her eyes off me. The lizard tattoo on her neck was asleep, and she was wearing her black backpack as usual. "Jean Carlo Hernández." Pats on the shoulder, and a big strong hug. "O Captain! My Captain!" he said in my ear, repeating a line from one of his favorite movies. Each medal was accompanied by a spring roll, which had to be dipped in a pot of sweet and sour sauce. "Esteban López." Tears in his eyes, and a tender smile. "Román Montero." The jealous, competitive look was gone. He shook my hand, squeezing it hard. On his forearm was a new tattoo: a tiny, broken drum. "María Victoria Tovar." Radiant smile. "Teach, thank you! You know I love you." "And I love you, Mimi." "Thank you very much. You don't know how much you mean to me. I'm being silly, sorry!" she confessed, wiping tears from her cheeks. There were three or four other students, those who make up the vast anonymous mass, but who, in their own way, without attracting attention, maintain an unwavering loyalty to their teachers. A lone medal remained on the dessert cart. The kids agreed to hold on to it for when Marcel Hidalgo regained his freedom. Jean Carlo put it in his pocket.

"That ends the first part of the Giménez-Ascanio-Wong graduation ceremony." The applause was deafening. The graduates threw their greasy napkins, stained with spring rolls, into the air, like they do with mortar board caps in all the gringo films. Then the noise, the hubbub, and the circulating began. There was shared laughter and brief but genuine happiness. Román went over to the music equipment built into the corner. A reggaeton came on. My knowledge of Caribbean music was quite limited; I could only distinguish between salsa and merengue. All those repetitive and tiresome rhythms that appeared at the turn of the century seemed equally nonsensical to me. I just liked the songs by Éxigo. The kids started dancing. Andrea and Jean Carlo were dancing on a table, making a hissing noise through their teeth. He grabbed her by the waist and pulled her toward him, bringing their bodies close, bringing their hips together, making the movements of animals in heat. Esteban and José Luis danced beside them, locked in a deep kiss. Román and Mimi completed the triangle, while a Puerto Rican poet named Ozuna sang ecstatically about the crazy thing that comes over him when he thinks about his girl. Mimi came up to the bar, took my hands, and led me onto the dance floor. I indulged them by making a fool of myself, letting myself get caught up in their fleeting joy. It had been months since I'd seen them like this, with the solace of a few minutes of peace. The graduation party at Giménez's bar gave them a moment of calm. Despite the brevity of the celebration, despite the fact that what they had hanging around their necks was a brass medal won in an inter-neighborhood softball tournament, they felt they had graduated with honors. They knew it was contrived, ridiculous, but they still enjoyed the overblown fantasy of their success. Ascanio and Wong joined the circle, raised their hands, and sang. I pretended to be tired and thirsty and went back to the bar. Señora Hernández was drinking an Aniversario rum. I asked her how she was feeling. She lied. The bruise on her forehead had turned green and some movements caused her pain, but she said she felt fine. "Thank you, Fernando." "I had nothing to do with this party. It was Ascanio and Wong's idea." "I don't mean for this, but for everything." "I'm just doing my job, Elena." "It's more than just doing your job and you know it. I don't know if you realize what you mean to them." Jean Carlo and Andrea's dance routine was perfect. They looked like professional Cuban salsa dancers. At one point, Jeanco tried to kiss her, but she dodged him. "My Gordo has been in love with that girl ever since he was little, but she has a heart of stone." We clinked our glasses. "You will say that that's just a mother's foolishness, that any woman who has given birth would feel the same way. But I know that my son has been called on to do something special. God protects him, watches over him, and cares for him. Marcel is in prison because he went back to help Jean Carlo. Soldiers from the National Guard were pursuing them through Chacaíto. Gordo slipped and fell. Marcel came back for him and helped him up. That's when they caught him. They shot him in the leg. 'Run, Jean Carlo, run!' was the last thing he said before they shoved Marcel into the back of the police van. The day Jacobo was killed, I was at home, ironing or something. I heard the explosion at the gas station. I felt something here, deep down in my chest. I went out onto the street, knowing that something was happening to my son. That's when I saw him surrounded by those bastards. I didn't think twice about it. I threw myself on him. Once again, God protected him. I know he has a mission in this world, though, at this moment, I don't know what it is. Only time will tell." The requiem of the poet called Ozuna faded out. Despite its melodic poverty, "*Vaina loca*" (Crazy Thing) was our Symphonie Fantastique, our Epic of Defeat, the most fleeting and transitory Ode to Joy.

• • •

"Senhor Saramago was a wise man. He always knew what was going to happen. He tried to warn us, but we didn't listen." Moreira ran his hand along the spines of the books in his library, found the one he was looking for, and opened it at random. "Here it is," he said, after a few minutes of reading it silently: "'This is not Portugal, it's something from another world, like a huge meteorite that fell to earth and in so doing split in two to let the water come gushing out.' See, now who would have thought the matter of the asteroid is nothing more than a return to the origins of our Mother Earth. Everything is written, Fernando. And not just in Lisbon. Believe me when I tell you there is some ingenious writer who knows very well what will happen to us, to you, to me, to this country. I have been alive a long time, dear friend. I have met many people. I have lived through happiness and regret. Nothing or no one could convince me that reality is random or that our fortunes, however insignificant they may seem, are not part of a larger plan. God knows where He is going. We don't. Uncertainty is our burden and our dilemma." Signs of hunger were evident on my gaunt face and scrawny body. Moreira offered me some bread and a bowl of *caldo verde*. He asked me if I had any new news about Portugal, but all I knew was what I'd heard on El Bus TV. Television was a puppet theater. Information about the disaster in Europe came through in dribs and drabs in the news. When social media was restored, control over everything that was said was tightened. The hashtags dedicated to the cataclysm disappeared. Only those tweets supporting the conspiracy theory of it being an orchestrated disaster were left untouched. The official line was the only window to the effects of the catastrophe, so we couldn't stay up to date on the decisions of the emergency summit in Braga, or the plans of the European Union to deal with the uncontrollable flow of refugees. Moreira's house was still my ivory tower, my favorite safe haven, the only place I felt I wouldn't be torn apart by loneliness.

"The return to Lisbon was the biggest disappointment in Agustina's life. The Revolution never thought to take into account people like us, returnees. When we arrived at Praça do Comércio, the carnations from the April Revolution were withered. Our illusions crumbled, blown away in the breeze. There was no place for us. After the fall of the Estado Novo, Agustina's attitude changed. Her antagonism toward others dissipated with the certainty that she would quickly resume her life in Portugal. She was convinced that her time in Caracas was nearing an end, and the idea of returning to Portugal made her feel less resentful of everything. But my Agustina did not realize that the world had moved on without her, that her youth had come to an end, and that her mysterious departure from Lisbon had raised multiple suspicions. Portugal had remained the same, barely marked by a patina of time. But the country had become politically more moderate. Newfound freedom breathed hope into people's hearts. Where oppression and despotism are the norm, where despotic rulers impose their names on the country, and apocryphal versions of its history are sanctioned with prison, it is difficult to entertain the hope of change or to think that life can be lived differently. But it was true. It had happened: the days of Salazar were over.

"I decided to accompany her to Lisbon, concerned about her well-being. If I had to let her go, I wanted to make sure she would have a place to stay, that she would make peace with her father, or that her old relationships at the university or the theater would allow her to find a profession. Our legal status was still uncertain. The marriage was a sham. In the eyes of God and men, I was still married to Lucía. Despite her mysterious release, Agustina had been a victim of the PIDE, and, in theory, she could seek compensation for damages before the courts that had been set up. In hindsight, what happened next wasn't surprising. It had just been overlooked in all the excitement.

"Agustina's old friends were cool toward her, put out by her unexpected return. One of the few people who met up with her told her that Arlindo was murdered by state security agents a few weeks after his arrest. His body showed up in the Parque Eduardo VII, with signs of torture. They claimed that it was suicide. A colleague from the theater recognized her in a restaurant on Rua da Prata. She came over to our table and spat in Agustina's face, called her a traitor, because everyone who knew her thought her sudden freedom had been bought. It was said that her father had pulled strings for her, that his influence had managed to save her, on the condition she betray her friends who were mixed up with the Portuguese Communist Party. Agustina's claims of innocence were dismissed. None of the survivors gave credence to her arguments. My wife was unable to convince her old friends that a PIDE officer had decided to release her for the sheer satisfaction of doing the right thing. We're not used to good faith, much less in times of dictatorship, when morale is low and the only thing that matters is one's own survival. The resentment from the past spilled over. Hypocrites weren't tolerated. Arlindo's younger brother met up with Agustina in the gardens of the Castelo de São Jorge. He accused her of being a collaborator. He threatened to initiate legal action against her. He told her that his family was aware of everything she had done and that they wouldn't rest until justice was served.

"While Agustina was confronting her own fate, coming to terms with having been expelled from paradise, I wandered around the outlying suburbs of Lisbon. And there I saw my lost youth, reflected in the shop windows, waiting for a life that had not been fulfilled, that had taken a U-turn. Many times, Fernando, the choices we make, the decisions we make, are a test set by God, over which we have no control. I never conceived of a life beyond Gouvinhas. Then, when I left Trás-os-Montes, I thought I had found my place in Lisbon. But suddenly I found myself aboard a ship, standing beside a girl who wanted to live fast, and who had become my wife as if by magic. Sometimes, I confess, I dreamed of the possibility of returning to my mountain town, of gathering a few chestnuts and offering them to the memory of my loved ones. But that country had ceased to be my country. Long before the devastation, Portugal was already a blur for me, a place I could only evoke through memory. Forgive my digression. Sadness is inevitable when we realize we can never return to the places where we were once happy. Let's go back to the year 1974. Join me on a walk through the cobblestoned streets of Lisbon. On that tour, I wondered what had become of Lucía. I was afraid of running into her and being admonished for cruelly abandoning her. I also wondered what would have become of my life if I had stayed with her. I took stock. I weighed up the many scenarios and was satisfied with how things had turned out. Between a ghost and a demon, the choice was not so difficult.

"When I returned to the hotel, Agustina was desperate. She told me about her encounters and the fallings-out she'd had. She knelt down and hugged my legs, unable to take in what was happening to her. How it hurt to see her suffer and not be able to do anything! Because, in all truth, Fernando, despite everything we had gone through, I had fallen in love with her. Nothing in this world interested me more than Agustina's happiness. I had long since resigned myself to her being estranged from me, to sleeping on the floor, but I loved her and I didn't like to see her sad. She didn't find what she was looking for. Her self-persecution led her nowhere. That trip was a coming apart, a radical splintering of her adult woman's soul. Visiting her father was also a disappointment. Old Urbano Gomes, ruined, brought down by debts, hardly recognized her. The knowledge that his most trusted man, his driver, his domestic servant, had run away with his only daughter, drove him crazy, even though it had saved her life. He had gone on without her, forgotten her. He felt nothing when he saw her again. The first thing he did was berate her for leaving without any warning and for abandoning her sick mother. The house was rundown. The years of splendor had ended with the disappearance of António de Oliveira Salazar. We walked through the Bairro Alto in silence. In the São Pedro de Alcântara garden, we sat on a bench. When I least expected it, Agustina dictated what our next steps should be: 'Let's go back to Caracas, Moreira. This isn't our home. We don't belong here.'

"On the return flight, something unexpected happened: Agustina took my hand and didn't let go of it until we landed at Maiquetía Airport. Lisbon vanished into the distance. It became tiny and invisible. Dark clouds veiled the sky, covering up the last vestiges of Europe. My young wife closed her eyes and moved her lips, as though in prayer. Years later, she confessed to me the curse she had made. Agustina pleaded for the destruction of Portugal, imploring God to blow it to pieces, to erase it from the map. Over the years, Senhor Almada Negreiros's "*A Cena do Ódio*" ("The Scene of Hate") would become her favorite poem. You know it, don't you? 'I am Medusa's rage and the sun's wrath!' Anger protected her from pain. A false but necessary anger. Contempt sometimes helps us to move on, to stay away from the things that hurt us and avoid responsibility for our mistakes. Anger is irrational and aggressive. Many times, it makes us say things we regret. If Agustina could ever have conceived that a stray asteroid would answer her prayer, she never would have dared to invoke it. She remained silent for the rest of the flight, staring blankly into the pitch black sky. For nine hours, she didn't let go of my hand. Before arriving in Caracas, she gently stroked my face. She looked at me differently. She wasn't the same person. Something had changed inside her. She leaned her head on my shoulder. She had made a decision. She had decided to follow the path she had been given, without looking back, without thinking that what she had lost was better than what she now had. 'Let's start over, Moreira. Forgive me for all the things I have done over the years. Forgive me for being the person I was. You don't deserve it. I promise you, from now on, everything will be different for us. I don't think it's that hard to be happy.'

"From that moment on, we became a true married couple. She allowed me to sleep beside her, to share her bed. Agustina gave me her love, but it's not proper for a gentleman to divulge the intimate details of his life with his beloved. You, who are a good and decent man, will understand my reservations. Suffice it to say that she loved me and that, to this day, despite her illness, she has made me feel happy and fortunate. Teolinda became her best friend, teaching her everything she knew about housekeeping, housework, and odd jobs. One night, while reading a novel by Raul Brandão, she recalled the morning in Trás-os-Montes when she wanted to teach me how to read. She suggested we take up from where we had left off last. In this way, night after night, we read together, until I fell asleep in the arms of the most beautiful woman in this world. Don't take offense, dear friend. I don't mean to disparage the beauty of your Tatiana by my appreciation of my own wife. All men in love believe their woman is the most beautiful in the world. And that fascination need not compete or offend, because as the proverb goes, 'beauty is in the eye of the beholder.' I had a hard time learning to read. It was difficult. At first, I would spend more than thirty minutes on a single paragraph, moving from syllable to syllable, slowly, until I understood the meaning of the sentences. I became a regular at the Divulgación bookstore, which my friend Sergio Alves had just opened at the Los Chaguaramos shopping mall. Some writers are more difficult than others. Senhor Saramago, for example. Oh, how he loves tongue twisters! I never understood the novels of Senhor Lobo Antunes or the poems of Herberto Hélder. And, between us, Carlos de Oliveira's novel *Finisterra* has neither beginning nor end. I prefer simple stories, like those of my beloved Eça de Queirós, who, during my years of learning to read, was my most precious friend and traveling companion.

"Lourenço's business flourished. The company enjoyed prestige among some old-money families. The Democratic Action Party put on lavish banquets every weekend, so the work was regular and well paid. My brother's relationship with Agustina was irredeemable, but they were at least civil with each other. The tension between them disappeared thanks to her *caldeiradas*. The success of the company allowed him to buy a large house in Colinas de Bello Monte, on Avenida Chama. The idea was to use the ground floor as an event space and rent out the patio for smaller celebrations. We stayed in the Prado de María. We were happy there. Plus, we were afraid of losing what we had found with each other, because with every move, Fernando, something is lost. Some places have a life of their own. The walls can suffer separation anxiety, and some belongings may resent our absence and hold a grudge.

"One day, when least expected, Agustina resumed her relationship with the theater. But this time taking on a discreet role, mostly behind the scenes. Señor Romeo Costea, whom she'd known back in the day during Curiel's productions, was her best friend and mentor. Chance brought them together in the Plaza de las Tres Gracias. That intolerable Petit Pois, as he was called, ran a theater school for young high school graduates and needed an assistant. Romeo was a small man, but he had the temperament of an angry titan. Agustina unintentionally became his right-hand man and the repository of his anger. He was a Frenchified Romanian. When I met him, he seemed a bit cocky, but Agustina was fascinated by his smugness. 'None of this avant-garde stuff!' He would shout angrily. 'They want to run before they can walk!' He said that the Venezuelans wanted to leapfrog Señor Shakespeare and make a beeline for Señor Genet, or move straight on to *Waiting for Godot* without having understood the plot of Señor Calderón de la Barca's *Life Is a Dream*. Señor Romeo was the one who taught Agustina the importance of classic theater, because during her formative years in Portugal she had also succumbed to the spell of modern drama, as if the world had begun with the Russian Revolution. Young people are always in such a hurry, dear friend. They look down on the past. Every generation believes itself superior to the previous one, and that they have God by the beard. Romeo's school was aimed at young people from the Libertador Municipality, working with the texts of Molière, Racine, and Corneille. I had never heard of those gentlemen. Agustina read them with interest and worked backstage in several school productions. She was comfortable with her new role. The dreams of the young people who appeared on the stage moved her in the way her own dreams had once done. Illusions don't die, Fernando; they're just transformed. We have to give up the flame or pass the baton at some point. If we have a goal and circumstances don't allow us to achieve it, we can continue to pursue it by helping the next generation. We can share our vision of the world with them. The young girl Agustina dreamed of being an artist. She had a puppet theater at her house in Gouvinhas. She knew the lines of all of Amália Rodrigues's films by heart. But when she didn't succeed, after she accepted the fact that she had missed her calling, she didn't fall apart. Instead, she did her best to ensure her students didn't make the same mistakes, and she helped them to soar. This is how we spent our best years, between

Petit Pois's workshops and our nightly reading sessions. She showed me love until the end, until her illness came between us.

"A few months before the first symptoms appeared, before we moved to Colinas de Bello Monte, something happened that changed our lives. We were given a mission. One afternoon in March, we received some unexpected visitors. As in one of Senhor Eça de Queirós's intricate plots, the true reason for Agustina's mysterious release from detention was revealed to us. We found out why her life had been spared. But it's late now, dear friend. Nighttime is approaching, and it can be dangerous for you to wander these cold streets. You will learn the end of the story at another time and, perhaps, in another place."

• • •

The unthinkable happened. They broke Ascanio's spirit. The flames destroyed his stationery store. A Molotov cocktail crashed through the window. The broken blinds caught fire, as did the photocopier (which hadn't worked for three years) and the reams of paper gone bad on the shelves. The *colectivos* fired shots into the air to intimidate and prevent the neighbors with fire extinguishers from putting out the flames. Ascanio decided to stay and burn with his store, but Wong prevented him from doing it. He dodged the flames, entered the premises, and dragged Ascanio out by force, kicking at the flames that licked at his legs. "My store! My store!" Ascanio's old smile was gone. Indignation warped his senses. Old Leonidas wanted to perish with his little world, surrounded by his collection of pencil sharpeners. Wong had to make an effort to hold him back. "My business, Antonio, my business!" The *colectivos* insulted Ascanio, calling him a thief and a traitor to the homeland, and threatened to shoot him. Later I learned that some unhappy neighbor had denounced him. The petitioner before SUNDDE (the consumer protection authority) stated that the old stationery store on Avenida Miguel Ángel was a front for *bachaqueo*, profiteering from the resale of basic goods and medicines, contravening the fair trade practices act. It was no secret to anyone that the stationery store was a place where things were resold illegally. But it was a place vital for our survival. We could do without salt and sugar, even coffee, but if we wanted to keep on living we had to feed ourselves something, tuna or pasta, and Ascanio spared no effort in scrounging up enough supplies to satisfy our needs. I know he made virtually nothing out of it. You could hardly call it profiteering. What little he made he spent on his friends, buying them drinks on the weekends at Giménez's bar, on the condition that they listen to his rants on freedom.

The flames consumed the building. A fire truck was parked on the corner, but it was out of water. Civil Defense officers ran from one side to the other, trying to evacuate the nearby apartments. A group of deadbeats and curious onlookers crossed their fingers hoping for a downpour. The flames threatened to spread throughout the block. Desperate, the head of the Baruta Fire Department ordered the neighbors to form a human chain with buckets down to the Guaire River. Buckets were tossed down from the open windows. Old people, children, and women formed a line to the polluted river banks, their hands getting smeared with shit. The fire spread to the La Espiga bakery. Security guards and the regular beggars who stood outside the Central Madeirense supermarket evacuated the customers inside. People ran down the street, holding on to their few belongings, as they watched the fire that was devouring Colinas de Bello Monte. The National Guard cordoned off the area. Two water cannons came down from the highway, drove onto the sidewalk, and put out the fire. The owner of the drugstore confronted the guardsmen over their delay in arriving and for being indifferent toward the *colectivos* responsible for the incident. The highest-ranking officer punched him in the gut and threw him headfirst into the back of a pickup truck. The furious, smoke-affected neighbors put their buckets down on the ground and began throwing lumps of shit at the patrol cars. The henchmen fled in disarray. The stationery store building collapsed. "My store! My store!" Ascanio repeated, tugging at Wong's sleeve with one hand and pointing with his other at the store that was no longer there. The water cannons went off in the direction of Las Mercedes, riding roughshod over everything, running over the elderly, turning the Avenida into a garbage dump.

As the days passed, the backwater returned to normal. The fury abated, ground down by weariness and hunger. After the fire, all that remained was a gaping black hole where the stationery store had once stood. The walls of the other stores were charred a yellow-brown color. The shit smeared over the concrete dissolved. The gutters were filled with debris. Worms worked their way down the drains. Avenida Miguel Ángel was a dirt road. And we got used to the smell, resigned to living the rest of our days in a toilet. The loss of the stationery store made survival difficult. The neighbors who'd informed on Ascanio were the first to regret having done so. The La Espiga, Sabrina, and Oh Lalá bakery ovens stopped working. The food supply was left in the hands of the most heartless *bachaqueros*. Young children were struck down by disease. At night, you could hear the desperate cries of newborns, sucking their anemic mothers' breasts dry. Babies abandoned in garbage cans satisfied the hunger of stray dogs. But despite the continuous degradation and relentless humiliation we weren't allowed to complain. The only way to survive was to keep going, as if nothing had happened, as if the loss of dignity was something common. There were no alternatives. We had to get used to all the rot, accept the intimidation by armed *colectivos,* keep our heads down, cling to our loved ones, and protect that fragment of happiness in the tiny bubble of our homes. If any neighbors dared to speak out and say that the situation was intolerable, they were taken to task for their pessimism, for their defeatist attitude. In rote-learned jargon, they were told that we lived in a privileged city blessed by Mount Ávila's shrouded summit.

Two weeks after the fire, La Sibila was officially expropriated. A SEBIN committee, presided over by Prepucio, handed me a misspelled document in which one Ministry of People's Power or other granted control of the premises to another Ministry of People's Power. The police kept Avenida Chama under surveillance. The area had experienced outbreaks of rioting in recent months. Drunken officers broke into La Sibila and ransacked it. They threw the old sets and props—Mother Courage's wagon and Richard III's castle painted in cartoon colors—onto the street. An armored vehicle sat parked in front of the entrance. They forced me to sign the occupation order and asked me about Moreira, the legal owner of the property. I lied and said he was unwell, to protect him. Neighbors silently formed a circle around La Sibila. Crestfallen and with tears in their eyes, the kids watched quietly as our theater was evicted and transformed into a barracks.

Jean Carlo's fist was clenched. I realized he had a rock in his hand. I approached him discreetly. I stood next to him and whispered into his ear. I could sense Alexander's eyes firmly fixed on us. "Don't even think about it, Jeanco, please," I begged. "This is not the time." "Then when?" he murmured. I didn't answer. I was afraid to tell him that the time would never come. We were in the same place where Jacobo had been shot. "It's not fair, Teach. We can't just sit around and do nothing. Enough is enough!" He raised his fist, with an irrepressible desire to kill. "Dammit Jeanco, listen to me! I'm not burying another student today. Drop the rock now!" Alexander approached, with his hands on his waist. Andrea's intervention prevented any bloodletting. She took Jean Carlo's arm, gently lowered it, took the rock from his hand, and put it in her pocket. She stood next to him and laced her fingers through his. I was slow to notice, but all the kids had joined hands: Mimi, Román, José Luis, Esteban, and a host of anonymous others. They encircled the armored vehicle. They weren't doing anything wrong, but I knew that Prepucio might interpret this harmless form of protest as a provocation. "Call off your guard dogs, Professor Morales, and tell them to go home if they don't want any problems," he warned smugly, showing me his FAL rifle. "I've had my eye on this fat kid for a while now," he said as he approached. My legs shaking with numbness, I walked to the center of the circle. One by one, I looked at their faces. I made a slight gesture. I raised my hand, snapped my fingers, and drew a straight line in the air with my finger, like we did in rehearsals. They interpreted the signal and let go of each other's hands. They started walking in the opposite direction, toward Avenida Miguel Ángel. "Damn, Morales! You've got them well trained!" He snorted with a laugh, pointing at my crotch. There was a wet patch of urine on my pants. The soldiers made fun of my weakness. "Ha, ha, ha. The dumbass pissed himself! You'd better check to see if you shat your pants, too!" They sang in chorus, throwing a roll of toilet paper in my face. I walked in the direction of my house while they continued to ridicule me. Some neighbors, mothers of former students, came out to meet me. They told me they could help me wash my clothes, because despite the cuts in supply, they had managed to fill more than six buckets with water.

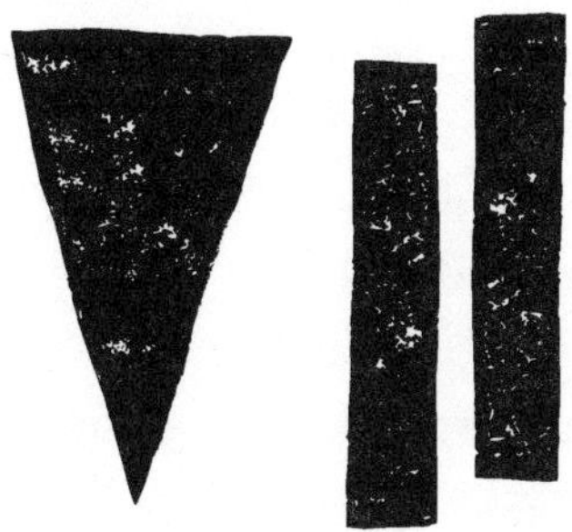

Offertory:
Choir of Souls in Purgatory

"Haja o que houver—Come What May."

THE RUMOR REACHED ME at Giménez's bar: Tatiana would be leaving the country, crossing the border through Colombia, bound for Chile. Our dirty laundry was not off-limits to others. Tati's deception was a source of ridicule for many gossipmongers on the block. My marriage had aroused the envy of all the mudslingers who shared their lives with plain homely women and couldn't bear to see one of their own with a pretty young girl. I don't remember which one gave me the news about Tatiana, but he was quite malicious in the way he did it. He asked me when we were leaving for Colombia, saying he'd heard Tatiana had bought bus tickets to San Cristóbal. I didn't fall for his game. I told him we were leaving soon. Stunned by what I had just learned, I walked over to her optometry shop. The PDV gas station was a huge crater. The rest of Las Mercedes was a desolate-looking avenue dotted with occasional displays of ostentation: gourmet restaurant façades, latest-model SUVs, armed bodyguards, and twentysomethings dressed in brand-name clothing, cocooned in their bubble of abundance. I walked to the dark, abandoned Paseo Las Mercedes shopping mall. Most of the stores were closed. A burst sewage pipe had flooded the basement, rendering the Trasnocho Cultural Center and El Buscón bookstore unusable. The smell of sewage permeated the whole place. The stairs leading up to the cinema and the theater were like the entrance to a sewer. The optometry shop was empty, with just a few cheap frames on display in the window. Yolanda became nervous when she saw me. She started scratching the palms of her hands, as she used to do during history tests all those years ago. "Teach!" she said, smiling. "I need to talk to Tatiana. It's important." She came out from behind the counter, took off her white optician's coat, and sat down. "Teach, it's none of my business. I don't want to get involved. I'm really sorry." "Tell me something: Is it true that Tatiana's leaving for Colombia?" An uncomfortable look crossed her face. She puffed and sighed, went into the office, searched for her phone, and dialed a number. She waited seven seconds: "Girl, deal with your own mess." She handed me the cell phone and left. All I had to do was hear Tati's voice to make everything go away. My anger dissipated. "How are you? We need to talk." "You're really something, Fernando!" She hung up without saying goodbye. I spent the rest of the afternoon at Giménez's bar, doing nothing, watching the preparations for a charity concert on TV. I went back to the apartment that night, cold and resigned to sleeplessness. When I passed by Ascanio's building, I thought I saw him leaning over the balcony, looking at the corner where his stationery shop used to be, with a look of resentment.

I found her sitting at the table with her back to me. The lit candle cast her shadow on the closed curtains. She had cut her hair. She was wearing new glasses and was looking through some documents. I hid my surprise. I walked over to her and kissed her on the cheek, as was our custom, before the end. I tried to caress her face, but she avoided me. She asked me to sit down opposite her. "You're right, Fernando. We need to talk." Her speech seemed rehearsed. The real content was in her empty gaze, in her body language, which revealed her annoyance. She claimed she never intended to hurt me. She asked for my forgiveness, but it was a disingenuous forgiveness, a means to an end. "If I hadn't forgiven you, I couldn't have gone on. I couldn't have healed," I said to her. She made as if to reply but stopped herself. My sense of calm seemed to offend her. "You're free. You always were. If you think you'll be better off in another country, if you think you can be happy with that boy, then go. If you're okay, if you're happy, a part of me will be satisfied. Your well-being will be my reward, even if we don't see each other again." She confirmed the rumors. Tomorrow afternoon she would be leaving for San Cristóbal by bus. She stopped pretending and showed me the documents lying on the table. Her voice broke and tears welled up in her eyes. She said that, despite the cost, it would be best to formalize the separation. She was breathing awkwardly, feigning a sense of ease. "Are you feeling okay?" She didn't answer. I stood up. I knelt down in front of her. This time, she didn't avoid my caresses. She placed her head on my shoulder. She made an effort to contain herself, but she burst into tears. Over and over, she professed her misery, her paranoia, her deep sorrow. "I can't stay here one more day. I really can't. I'll go crazy. This isn't life, not for you or for me. It wasn't you. It was never you. What I did, it wasn't to hurt you. . . . Dammit Fer, you're the best guy I've ever known." A gust of wind came in through the half-open window and blew out the candle on the table. The oil lamps in the kitchen cast a dim light. "I want you to do something for me," she added, wiping her eyes. "Get out of this country. Build your life somewhere else. You have a lot to give, Fernando. You can't rot here. This city is doomed. You have a talent I don't know how to describe. The kids love you. They learn things with you. In any other country, you could rebuild your life, get ahead, meet someone, and have a family." How could I make her understand I wasn't interested in meeting anyone else, that the only person I wanted to have a family with was her? "Thank Christ we didn't have any kids," she said, putting a lid on my inner monologue. "Can you imagine it? Do you know what it would be like to raise a child in this shithole?" I asked her about her travel plans, as I was worried about her safety. She told me she'd paid a fortune for the passport, and that she and a group of friends had raised the money together to cover the transport costs. They had rented a private bus that would take them to the border. She had places she could stay in Lima, Santiago, and Buenos Aires, but she hadn't made a decision yet. "It won't be easy, Tati." "I know, but anything is better than dying of sadness or waiting to be killed. What are you laughing at?" "You and me. It may be over between us, but we were happy together. We came far together. We had something real. If you need me someday, if things don't go well, if you want to come back, this will always be your home. This tiny apartment that you never liked because you said it smelled musty, it will always be your home. Don't worry about me, I'll be fine." I brushed her cheek with my hand. She kissed the inside of my damp palm. "Tell me one thing, just one thing. Óscar Cáceres? Why him? Unless you've done a one-eighty, I would venture to say he's not your type at all, that you have nothing in common. Did you really fall in love with him?" "No, you're right. Óscar meant nothing—*means* nothing—to me. It could have been anyone. All I needed was an excuse to get out of here, to make you realize we had no future. It was never you, Fernando." She got up, grabbed her purse, and slung it over her shoulder. *Don't go. Please don't go.* I silenced my humiliation. I clasped my hands around her neck and attempted to kiss her. At first she tried to pull away, but seconds later, her lips sought mine. Her mouth was dry and her breath smelled of cigarettes. We pressed closer together, our tongues circling each other, moving in sync. Her hand reached for my crotch. She wanted to undo my belt. I pulled away in disgust. Despite my forgiveness, the wounds were still raw. "I never had to penetrate you to make love to you." She backed away from me, angry. "Dammit Fernando, why do you have to be so intense? What do you want then? Tell me what you want?" "Is that why you came here? 'Oh that poor, sad guy! I feel so sorry for him. I'll give him a pity-fuck and then leave, so he won't be sad!'" She walked over to the door. "Wait!" I cried. "Be straight and just tell me what you want," she said. We stared at each other wide-eyed. A heavy silence hung between us. "Do you really want to know? To watch you sleep." We both chuckled. She came back into the living room. She threw her purse on the table and sat down on the sofa. She covered her face with her hands, still laughing, but interrupting her laughter with long puffs of air. "You're leaving tomorrow, right? You've slept in this apartment for the last ten years. One more night won't make a difference. I'm serious, Tati. Stay the night and sleep here with me." The electricity came back on. The lightbulb in the room exploded. The bathroom suddenly lit up, flickering. Tatiana composed herself, got up, and went into the kitchen. She made a phone call. I couldn't hear what she was saying. She spoke in whispers. Five minutes later, she came back into the living room. "Okay, Fer. What do you have to drink?"

For what seemed like an inexhaustible length of time, accompanied by a bottle of Sansón cooking wine, we went back in time to the Greenwich bar. We talked quietly, like old friends, about the traps of living together. It was cold. We took out a blanket (the green blanket we had bought on our vacation in La Puerta). The memories of our happy times together were genuine. We recounted the best moments of our relationship, describing them from each other's point of view, agreeing on the essence, on the core aspects of our relationship that had once led us to believe we would watch each other grow old together. I teased her about her poor housekeeping skills, her inedible rice, and her inability to distinguish parsley from oregano. We were surprised by the sunrise, pink and gray, orange and black, behind a blanket of thick, immovable clouds. We were drunk and yawning. Our faces were very close. "I love you, Fernando." "And I love you, Tati." "In a different place, we would have had better luck, but we're not made to survive in hell. Take good care of yourself, okay? Promise me." "You too. I hope life gives you what I didn't know how to give. Go, go and dazzle the world, like you once dazzled me." Her eyes closed. She lay back on the sofa, propping her head on a cushion. I sat down to look at her, to savor her eyes, her nose, her mouth, her perfect ears. "Sing me a song." "Which one?" "I don't know, anyone you like," she whispered sleepily. It had been a long time since I'd picked a song from the salsa erótica playlist. Her breathing gradually became slower. She stretched, yawning, her warm breath showering my face. I remembered some lyrics that took me back on a journey through time. Tatiana was wrapped in a yellow apron that had the Beco department store logo on it. We were making a birthday cake. She was happy and radiant. And she asked me to put that song on the iPod. With our hands covered with flour, we danced in the hallway. We ended up making love on the floor. The cake burned. Like all those manufactured tunes, I memorized it by sheer dint of repetition every time it was her turn to cook or when we were in the car together. I had forgotten the melody, so I improvised. In a hoarse, rough, out-of-tune voice, I murmured the song into her ear. Our story began to be told in reverse, from the first moment I noticed her pulling away from me back to when it all began, at a bar in Altamira. Images of her flashed through my mind. I saw her emerging from the shower, with her hair wet and wrapped in a towel; laughing in the middle of an orgasm; running late for work, eating breakfast standing up, her hands covered in jam; singing songs by Guaco with Yolanda, both of them drunk, at some forgotten Christmas party; taking her temperature when she was sick, doing what I could to ease her fever; reading and underlining passages in the Stendhal book; coming home from work, desperate to kiss me and tell me about her shitty day. I was there, with a lover's enthusiasm, the day she tried to fry some *tequeños* and the pan caught fire, because they'd sold us rancid oil. Laughter gave way to stress and strain, money worries, shortages, despair at the endless lines, fear of being out at night and the risk of getting mugged. And I realized then how we became estranged, how I lost her, how things got out of hand, how our love was thwarted and doomed. "But now the crisis has passed and the bad times are behind us, my darling . . ." I echoed some of the words from the last verse. I kissed her forehead. "Let's do what our heart says. Good luck, my love. Rest well. And remember, whatever happens, I will always wait for you."

I was awakened by the pipes banging. The water had come back on. It came out strong, brown, full of insects, cloudy and hot, but liquid. I had a stuffy nose. The pillow was dusty. Tatiana left without saying goodbye. She shut the door. I pretended to be asleep. She made a move to approach me, but then stopped midway, afraid, perhaps, that I would ask her to stay. I got up awkwardly. She left me a note on the table: "You know that I loved you. Somehow, you'll always be with me. Thanks a million. I hope you find someone better than me." The urge to urinate sent me to the bathroom. A yellowish stool was floating in the toilet bowl, while a trickle of water was filling up the tank. The gushing stream of piss made the stool spin in circles. I looked out the window. I saw her get into a Corsa. She kissed the driver on the lips, leaned back in the passenger seat, and then the car sped off. I never imagined that our story would end that way. That the last images I would have of her would be the random verses of a song by Grupo Niche and the lingering smell of her shit.

• • •

The horizon was a curved line lit with distant flares. Bursts of machine-gun fire interrupted the loud percussive sounds of the *guacharacas*. On the afternoon of my final visit to Moreira, he wanted to go out. When I arrived at his apartment, Señora Agustina was in the middle of the room, dressed, and seated in the wheelchair. Pantera picked us up in the parking lot. Moreira asked him to take us somewhere outdoors. He didn't want to tell me the end of his story in the solitude of his house. There weren't many places to go. The city was under siege. There were roadblocks at every corner. The mountain was our only alternative. The winding roads were deserted; the surrounding farms, withered and abandoned. Valle Arriba was a ghost town. While driving, we didn't come across a single person, just rusted cars stranded on four concrete blocks. Despite the warnings of Pantera, who was afraid we would be robbed, we stopped at the lookout in La Alameda. The Prados del Este Highway down below in the distance was a huge battlefield. I pushed the wheelchair to the center of the plaza. We contemplated the landscape, the black smoke, the orange clouds, polluted by gases. The three of us, side by side, observed the destruction of our little world. Moreira took Agustina's hand and wiped her lips. Before starting, he gave me a broad smile.

"One afternoon in March, during our last few days in the Prado de María, a couple from Brazil paid us a visit. They wanted to meet my wife. Their name was Rodrigues, and they were originally from the Alentejo region in Portugal. And they told us about a man named Aquilino Moraes. The name meant nothing to us, but when Agustina saw the photographs, she recognized him as the PIDE officer who had saved her life. We knew, then, that her case had not been an exception. That officer's compassion helped many people escape prison and sometimes death. His PIDE uniform did not prevent him from having a bit of humanity. The Rodrigueses told us they had counted up more than thirty people who, over a period of fifteen years, had been saved thanks to the officer's timely intercession. He was not selective in who he chose to help. He was guided purely by chance. When circumstances permitted, he made the necessary arrangements to free the prisoners behind his superiors' backs. The Carnation Revolution, however, sentenced him to ostracism. The truth commissions that were formed after the fall of the Estado Novo blacklisted him as one of Salazar's suspected henchmen. When the PIDE headquarters were ransacked, information found there provided the basis for him to be charged for crimes in a court of justice. But he disappeared without a trace before any charges were made. The Rodrigueses began an investigation to find his whereabouts, to look him in the face and to ask him why he'd chosen them, why he'd saved their lives. Their investigations proved to be revealing. They hadn't been the only ones he'd saved. The arbitrary intervention of that officer prevented countless crimes and torture. The list of those who'd been protected by Moraes was long, and it included Portuguese nationals residing in Mexico, Costa Rica, Colombia, Peru, Brazil, Argentina, and Venezuela. The Alentejan couple's intention was to find him in order to bring his legacy to light. Agustina listened to the story, absorbed, silently reconstructing the dramatic days of her incarceration. She had erased her period of imprisonment from her memory. She didn't like thinking about Portugal, much less her brief stay in prison. She shared her experience with them and promised to help them in their search. The couple's investigation, however, drew a blank. The testimonies of the victims scattered across Latin America piled up, but the hero's fate remained an enigma. The Rodrigueses returned to Brazil, leaving behind unfinished business, something we knew we had to face.

That was when the first symptoms appeared: the trembling in the hands, the loss of hearing. The illness slowly took over Agustina's body, so we weren't able to help with the investigation to locate our savior. My wife knew her fate. She had seen her grandmother and mother wither in the same way, so she didn't resist. There was no way to fight against the inevitable.

"Around that time, Lourenço and Teolinda left Venezuela. My brother went back to Portugal. He wasn't rich, but with the money he'd earned from the events company, he could buy his own Gouvinhas. He didn't like what was happening in Caracas. He sensed the imminent disaster, the gradual and invisible destruction of our adopted country. He wasn't a man of faith, but on the day of his departure he told me he'd had a dream. He met the devil, who'd planted himself atop Mount Ávila and who warned him he'd come to stay. They moved to Lisbon. Lourenço tried to settle back in the Marão, but it's impossible to return to the places one grew up in without melancholy laying down a trap. The absences from the past are painful. Memory and reality often clash. Before he left, my brother put the house on Avenida Chama in my name and paid me the remainder of my earnings. After they left, we would talk on the phone during the holidays. Once a year he sent us a box of books, Portuguese authors who were unknown in the Spanish-speaking world, and with whom Agustina and I maintained our reading sessions and our unshakeable love for the Portuguese land. The wonderful novel *Galveias* was one of his last gifts to us. Oh! If only the world listened more closely to writers, we would have better luck. I don't know how it happened, but that young novelist, José Luís Peixoto, had already seen the comet pass. He tried to warn us, but we didn't take him seriously.

"The house on Avenida Chama was too big for us. The stairs were an ordeal. We looked for another place to live, and that was when we found a small apartment in the Centro Polo, where we're living out our last days. Agustina's illness put an end to many projects. She wanted to form her own theater school, to establish a name of her own, independent of her mentor, Romeo Costea. A few months before Agustina lost her faculties, she proposed turning the old house on Avenida Chama into a cultural center. She wanted to call it "La Sibila," in honor of her favorite novel. We drafted a program of the center's activities, but the ferocity of her illness killed off our efforts. Agustina's health rapidly faded, making daily life an ordeal, turning basic routines into excruciating burdens." A distant explosion interrupted Moreira's story. A part of Mount Ávila was ablaze, as if a waterfall of gasoline was pouring down from the invisible summit. "Before she lost her powers of expression, with the last glimmers of lucidity, my wife asked me to promise two things: that I not abandon the idea of La Sibila and that I find the man who'd saved her life. I had to look him in the face and thank him, and in the event that he needed help, to do my best to help him. That was the last time she managed to articulate something meaningful. After that came the babbling, the noises, the vague moans. I won't describe the details of our goodbye. The goodbye between two lovers is a private matter.

"My wife's last wishes were my most committed crusade. I tried, without success, to get the theater school off the ground. I needed to find someone competent, someone capable of taking on this task, but I didn't know how to go about it. I tried to apply for the permits at the mayor's office, but the red tape was overwhelming. The search for

Aquilino Moraes proved easier. In a telephone conversation with the Rodrigues couple, I inquired about their most recent findings. They had sufficient reason to believe that Moraes lived in Venezuela and that he'd chosen Caracas as his place of refuge. The information was vague. I had little expectation of finding him, but through a contact at the events company, an old military man who had a managerial position at SAIME, I learned that three people by the name of Aquilino Moraes lived or had lived in Caracas. The first one, in Los Rosales, was the owner of a small amusement park; the second one, in Urbina, was an old businessman sick with gout; and the third one lived in La Candelaria, near the Guernica restaurant. The phone number I had wasn't working, so I decided to pay him a visit. I was received by an elderly woman, who introduced herself as his sister-in-law. She invited me into her house and told me the story of the unfortunate Aquilino. She didn't know when he arrived in Venezuela, but she told me her younger sister had fallen in love with him. They met at the Quinta Crespo market, where her sister worked in a stall and he was a fish delivery man. They never married, but they had a son. When his son's birth was being registered, the clerks at the Births Registry Office didn't know better than to spell his surname in its Spanish version. Moraes became Morales. Rosaura, the lady with whom I spoke, told me that Aquilino was a man of few words. That he was seemingly embittered and overshadowed by guilt. He never talked about his past, but she sensed he was carrying a heavy weight inside him, because some nights, she saw him clutching a bottle of whiskey and heard him weeping and wailing. His bad conscience had pushed him to the edge. During the tragic events of 1989, when furious protesters seized the streets of Venezuela, Aquilino Moraes put a shotgun to his head and killed himself. Rosaura's sister couldn't bear the loss. The death of loved ones can sometimes bring out the worst in us. When all hope of happiness is lost, our hearts can become a breeding ground for anger and resentment. The conversation meandered onto different topics. We formed a connection. We liked each other. We shared a coffee and some shortcake. That's when I saw the photo of Moraes's son. Rosaura told me about you, Fernando. She gave me your address. She informed me that you lived in Colinas de Bello Monte and that you were a high school teacher. In Giménez's bar, I learned that long ago, together with a friend of yours, you had tried to set up a cultural center in the municipality, but that discussions with the Mayor of Baruta remained fruitless. You yourself didn't have the financial resources for it. Call it coincidence or chance if you like, but I think of it as fate. This old Portuguese man from Trás-os-Montes prefers to believe that God had a plan to bring us together."

The implications of Moreira's revelations didn't sink in until he finished his account. We were still standing at the La Alameda lookout, staring out at a sinister horizon. He spun the wheelchair around to face me, taking the sick woman's head in his hands and wiping the trickle of saliva at the edges of her lips. "My darling Agustina, this is the son of the man who saved your life. I have tried to help him with what little we have, just as you asked me to. But reality is harsh, and, in truth, I haven't been able to do much for him. I hope you can forgive me. His name is Fernando and he is a good person, like his father. My dear friend Fernando, may I present my wife to you, Agustina." He raised her lifeless hand and forced me to take it. "Don't be afraid, speak openly to her. She will understand. Somehow she understands. I have kept my word, I have fulfilled my mission. There's not much left for me to do in this world but wait for the end. If you wish, you can rest in peace now my darling, whenever you want. But if you prefer to wait, I will continue reading to you every night, as we have done all this time."

We stared at the battle going on down below, listening to the bullets echoing in the distance. The cold and weightless hand of the sick woman was still clamped in mine. My memories flickered back to the shadow of a man I barely remembered, and my eyes filled with tears. "I would have liked to ask your father why he chose to save Agustina. What made him help so many people? Why did he disobey his superiors? How many were there he wanted to save and couldn't? What made him ignore Salazar and risk his own neck for the lives of complete strangers? Today, dear friend, generations of Portuguese exist thanks to him disobeying and intervening. His act of sabotage is part of the living memory of our Portugal that has disappeared. Despite being told that harm is necessary, people can always choose not to harm others, Fernando. Not all perpetrators lack souls. Some end up becoming their own executioners. Senhor Torga put it well: 'Men's hearts, however hard they may be, always have a weak spot for some softness to find its way in.'" "Why didn't you tell me this earlier, Moreira? Why haven't you told me about this before?" "I don't know. It wasn't the right time. I'm not the master of ceremonies here. I'm not the one who calls the shots. The one who calls the shots is sitting behind those black clouds. Oh, how ingenious! An asteroid had to wipe out half of Portugal for you to deign to visit me." "What's the point of all this? What was your plan, Moreira?" I pointed to the highway, the black smoke, and the wall of fire crossing

Mount Ávila. "If your God exists, then he is sick." "Humanity will prevail, dear friend; it always prevails, never doubt that. As long as there are men like your father, who choose life, in spite of their circumstances, we will have hope."

Moreira noticed my skepticism, my sarcastic smile. "Don't be so hard on yourself. In your own way, you are a hero." A snort of laughter escaped me. I appreciated his attempt to make me feel better, but I rejected his line of thought. "I'm just a fool; a dreamer without dreams." Moreira, masterful interpreter of my sadness, challenged my outburst. "The kids, Fernando! Don't forget the kids. The work you do with them is admirable. Your profession is admirable. Don't underestimate your efforts. You have made an impression on the lives of many of those young people who are out there, dying on the streets, fighting for their freedom. And they will get it, Fernando, they will succeed one day. They always do. That is what history teaches us. The people will win the battle, for it is their destiny. The ordinary person doesn't know how difficult it is to inspire the afflicted, to raise the spirits of the hopeless and tell them that, even though it hurts to breathe, it's worth it to go on living. Have patience with time, Fernando. Believe me, someday one of those kids will achieve something important: they will discover a vaccine, compose a symphony, win an Olympic medal, or pass a law that will make this world a fairer place. And when that happens, when they take stock, they will say to themselves, 'If it weren't for what my teacher Fernando taught me, I would not have succeeded.'" "They will achieve nothing, Moreira. While we stand here talking, they're being killed or violated in El Helicoide prison. I'm not proud of my work. On the contrary, I feel a deep regret for encouraging them to dream, for reinforcing illusions that will lead nowhere, because they're unattainable, because this country is finished. It stopped existing a long time ago. We are the last survivors, but we are doomed." "There is still time to do something about it." "And what am I supposed to do?" "I don't know. You're the teacher. I'm just an illiterate man from Trás-os-Montes, a stand-in chosen by God to help you find your way." A woman's desperate, tortured screams carried over from the highway. The echo, turned into a howl, pierced through us. "Oh, poor country, dear friend!" A flash of lightning appeared in the overcast sky. "Soon the fog will pass, fear not. Let me share a few words with you, a beautiful poem by Senhor Pessoa. He wrote it as a farewell to Portugal, anticipating what would happen in this cursed year. It's an inspiring, prophetic message. His verses are just as pertinent to the hills of Caracas that are so similar to those of our land. Poets are generous souls. You look on at the suffering city below and reflect on what I have just told you." Agustina's inert body, bent over in the wheelchair, was between us. Her fingers had slipped from my hand. Moreira seemed to be remembering something. He whispered to himself in Portuguese, while tear gas exploded in the distance, swirling like a sandstorm in the sky above Caracas. Then, all of a sudden, after it started to drizzle, he recited: "Not King nor law, nor peace nor war, / Defines in outline or in substance / The tarnished brilliance of this land / Called Portugal, now come to grief— / A brilliance lacking luster, spark / Encircles like the will-o'-the-wisp." He looked down at the ground, tired, making an effort to maintain his implausible optimism. "None knows what it is he wants. / None knows what is in his soul, / Nor yet knows what's good or ill. / (What distant anguish echoes here?) / All's uncertain, nears its end. / All's fragmented, nothing's whole. / Oh Portugal, today you are the fog . . ." The downpour started. Pantera came over with an umbrella. Agustina and Moreira returned to the car. I stayed at the lookout with my eyes closed, stinging and burning from the acid rain, and I tried to talk to God, infuriated by His silence and His complete indifference.

• • •

I woke up late, around noon. It was cold, but it was the silence that was most chilling. I headed over to the bar. Someone was moving out of Ascanio's building. Two people were loading a sofa onto the back of a pickup truck parked in the drive. Giménez was cleaning the beer filters. On the TV, they were broadcasting a concert commemorating the first anniversary of the Portuguese tragedy: *Lisbon Forever*. "They really fooled us with that end of the world stuff! And yet here we still are. A real shame!" He served me a bowl of soup, with bubbles of fat floating on the surface. I dunked a piece of bread in the orange liquid. "Another one who's leaving," I said indifferently, to make conversation. Giménez creased his brow, confused. I told him about the pickup truck parked across the street. He shook his head. "What, didn't you hear? Ascanio hanged himself." I almost choked on my soup. "There were no ambulances to come and take his body away. What you saw wasn't a sofa. It was Leonidas's body wrapped in a blanket." I pushed the bowl away. "May the good Ascanio rest in peace!" said Giménez, going back to cleaning the worn-out beer filters again. I leaned over the bar and turned up the volume on the TV. U2 was singing an elegy. The occasional sound of a grenade exploding or a burst of shrapnel came from the highway. The dead spoke up: little Jacobo banged on his drum, calling out my name. An unfamiliar, faceless man put a shotgun in my hand.

Moreira's revelations made my dilemma more painful. Lady Gaga brought me out of my reverie. Her operatic song—voice and piano, almost a cappella—silenced Germany. The kids' faces asked me for help. They needed me. Something inside me told me I had to do something for them, to try to save them, as my father had done for the innocent people he was forced to condemn. Anguish consumed me. My hives flared up all over my body. My gums were bleeding, and I had a rash on my wrists. They couldn't continue killing them. One side or the other had to come to realize that the only thing we were achieving was our total annihilation. A flash of lucidity came over me. I accepted Moreira's point of view. I finally understood what he meant. The sound of guitar chords caused a lump in my throat. The concert closed with the Portuguese group Madredeus, whose members had survived the catastrophe because they were on a reunion tour in Eastern Europe at the time the asteroid struck. I didn't know who Teresa Salgueiro was, but when I heard her ballad, I had the impression we'd been friends for years and that, somehow, we had written the song together. Close-up on the screen: huge tears in the eyes of a woman in mourning. Silence in Berlin. There was a single spotlight on stage, encircling the performer. "*Haja o que houver*" (Come What May) was an exhortation, a "get up and keep going" song with which I gathered enough strength to confront my childish fears. The melody was a road map to point the way through. A declaration that no matter what happened, everything would be okay. That I would be here and would wait for my love, as the song vowed.

I met Wong in the middle of the street. He had Ascanio's wine-colored sweater wrapped around one hand and a ridiculous bamboo steamer lid as a shield in the other. He told me about the rumors he'd overheard in the lines at the supermarkets. Maracaibo and Valencia were in open rebellion. An overthrow was imminent. The Portuguese tragedy had tipped the balance in favor of the liberation of Venezuela. The European Union was unable to contain the human tides who had escaped from hell. Diseases decimated survivors and epidemics spread across the continent. As in the days of Vasco da Gama, Portuguese migrants had begun the reconquest of Latin America. Intercontinental travel from English seaports became the most sought-after route for salvation across the Atlantic. Orphaned and destitute Portuguese people crossed the ocean in search of a new life. The institutional anarchy in Venezuela made it difficult for humanitarian organizations to deal with the influx of environmental refugees from Portugal. We had long since stopped believing in the murmurs of freedom, but this time, there was a vague hint that the Revolution's hours were numbered. When Venezolana de Televisión, the main state channel, unexpectedly interrupted its broadcasts, millions of people took to the streets of Caracas. The flyover above the highway became a sea of white T-shirts and tattered flags. They marched in complete silence, their sickly pale faces disfigured by malnutrition. There was no chanting or cheering, as in the days of the festive protests when the mask of joy was on display all around. For the first time since the start of the conflict, the military cordon the Armed Forces usually set up near El Rosal had been broken through. The protesters charged through the roadblock, forcing the military to retreat to the city center. Huge swells of people came from Valle-Coche, from Paraíso, and Montalbán. The last army stronghold had barricaded itself under the overpass above Central University, shooting to kill at everything around them. The protestors' hopes were still somewhat subdued. We did not have sufficient reason to believe. We had come close on other occasions. Freedom had been within our grasp, only for us to then be deceived and humiliated by spurious agreements, council plans, dishonest elections, useless dialogues, and invisible negotiations between opportunistic and corrupt leaders. The probability of fresh disappointment was greater than the expectation of success.

When I reached the main avenue of Colinas de Bello Monte, the Guaire River was about to overflow. I risked crossing the bridge, overcoming my fear of the shotgun blasts battering my eardrums, determined to get to the other side. At the intersection, an overturned water cannon emitted gray smoke and the smell of burnt flesh. Two National Guardsmen were on fire in the front seat. They had no skin. They were wearing a uniform of flames. A naked body with its testicles cut off hung from the broken traffic lights. The man's face was familiar to me. Alexander—Prepucio—swayed in the breeze. Stray dogs kept a watchful eye on him, nipping at his ankles, eagerly drinking the blood that dripped from his blue legs. I wondered why he had tried to destroy us. I couldn't recall ever having done him any harm or having sinned by omission. Perhaps if I had been more attentive to his childhood grief, if I hadn't underestimated his level of discomfort, we would have avoided the senselessness of his fury.

The bridge over the river looked like Charon's boat, made of cheap asphalt. The concrete block was about to collapse. There were more corpses than shit in the Guaire River. The murky stream carried myriad humans and debris. The normally brown water had turned red. The clearings along the highway had become makeshift hospitals, in which the *Cascos Verdes*, the Green Cross volunteer medics, piled up the maimed. Furious mothers threw rocks at any soldiers they encountered, looting their patrol cars and armored vehicles. I let myself be carried along by the crowd, following the path of those who were sick with rage. Dark clouds made it impossible to see the top of Mount Ávila. The ground was littered with glass shards and bullet casings. The Aladdin Hotel on the side of the road was burning. The fire had started on the first floor, but the flames had reached the rooftop, melting the kitsch minarets on top of the building. A couple was having sex on the fifth-floor landing of the spiral stairs. Resigned to perishing in the flames, they prepared to sacrifice themselves at the point of sexual climax, risking suffocation for an orgasm. No one paid attention to them. Their poignancy was a playful metaphor for us Venezuelans: momentary enjoyment was more enticing than the possibility of being saved.

The men and women of my generation progressed through inertia. Uncertainty maintained their sluggish, expectant but furtive steps. The older people could not contain their frustration, the pain of their open wounds, of all they had lost. But the young people, the kids with gaunt and malnourished features, whose childhood had been stolen, walked with more determination. I recognized several former students, classmates, and confidantes. "Teach!" they shouted, beaming faces flushed with fatigue. I made out the Azpurua brothers, along with Arias, Bastardo, Bejarano, Castro, Cifuentes, Córdova, Egan, Fernández, Granados, Heredia, López, Losada, Maita, Manrique, Méndez, Sánchez, Sandoval, Padrón, Pellico, Porras, Quirós, Torres, Valdés, Vera. Twenty years of service that had spawned miserable and diseased faces. They had managed to survive, to overcome the effects of the fight to the death. And I thought of all those who had left the country, driven from their birthplace. In the midst of the tumult, I recognized the kids from the La Caja de Fósforos Theater. Many of them had taken their first steps in La Sibila. I came across some of my colleagues, too, the old teachers from the Instituto Atenas, from Santo Tomás de Villanueva, Fray Luis de León, and Promesas Patrias, indomitable warriors who had chosen to fight their battles in the classroom. Julia was among them, haggard, her clothes tattered and torn. We didn't exchange any words. I kissed her lightly on the cheek and turned away from her, as I used to do after our failed attempts at bonding.

The putrid smell of rotting flesh hit me as I made my way to Plaza Venezuela. The old Zona Rental fairgrounds and the half-empty Banco Bicentenario covered market area were unsanitary wastelands, infested with hungry rats and snakes. The corpses of military personnel as well as protesters had been thrown indiscriminately into the ditches, one on top of the other, forming a pyre that gave off green smoke. Frantic people gathered around the statue of María Lionza. Some women lifted the lifeless bodies of their young children up in the air, waiting for a miracle. Others made profane offerings to the goddess. Most were standing at the base of the monument. They had their eyes closed, their hands covering their ears. "Enough! Dear Lord, please, no more!" they wailed loudly. The entrances to Central University were blocked. A bomb had destroyed the bridge. The only way to move through to the center was to scale the rubble or skirt around it along the banks of the Guaire River. The mural by the artist Pedro León Zapata had disappeared. There was only a shard of red ceramic rubble in which the ears of Simón Rodríguez could be made out. A gap in the fence gave access to the botanical garden. The flames had consumed the orchid collection, the palm trees, and the trunks of the apamate trees. There was nothing left of the vegetation, just a black patch in the center of which seven blue macaws had been slain and arranged in a triangle. The chaotic crowds made it impossible to move. Groups coming from Santa Monica and the west had merged into a mass. Armies of ordinary people had converged under the twin towers of the Parque Central Complex. There was no way through to Avenida Bolívar. Four incinerated armored vehicles blocked access to the tunnel. The last line of defense of the Revolution was holed up in front of the Teresa Carreño Theater, and what was left of the army was stationed on Avenida México. They had formed an impenetrable trench. There were no hierarchies or privileges, only the will of the strongest prevailed. There was a confusion of National Guard, SEBIN, and municipal police uniforms. Some began to desert and sought to become invisible in the masses.

Fatigue and fear prevented further attacks. The *Cascos Verdes* were handing out bottled water and transporting the wounded on ice cream carts. It was difficult to push through to the head of the march, but I had to find the kids. I had to tell them we had a chance. I knew they would be at the front. After Jacobo's death, they had no qualms about risking their lives. They hurled Molotov cocktails at the water cannons like experienced kamikazes, together with the street kids hooked on glue-sniffing. The vanguard was made up of a mob of defenseless kids who had lost their fear of death. I shoved in among them. Jean Carlo called out my name. He had a broken leg, with a stick for a splint. He raised his arm: "Teach!" We hadn't seen each other since La Sibila was closed down, when he threatened to lay down his life. He pointed toward Plaza Venezuela. La Tumba was in flames. He told me a riot had broken out in the prison and that the prisoners had escaped. The same thing had happened at El Helicoide prison. Andrea, Esteban, and José Luis were standing a bit farther away, covered in blood and dust from the sandbags, but alive and in one piece. The line of defense was a wall of sand-filled backpacks, tin shields, and decomposing bodies—bloated teenagers, whose faces were obscured by balaclavas. The survivors sharpened rocks, removed the powder from firecrackers, and poured gasoline into empty bottles.

Mimi was at the shoulder of the road, kneeling down and talking to a dying man. Román had an open abdominal wound from which a part of his intestines poked through. A pool of black blood had formed around María Victoria. Román's amber eyes were fixed on her face, impassive, calm, as if Mimi's gaze had an immediate soothing effect. She stroked his stained temples, kissed him on the head, and seemed to lull him with a joke or a lullaby. She pressed Jacobo's tattered flag against the wound, trying to stem the massive bleeding. His left foot began to move, stimulated by reflexes. Román spluttered, trying to speak, but his words came out in an unintelligible stream, drowned in a bloody coughing fit. He clutched at his T-shirt, and then his fist just went slack over his belly. He let out his final death rattle, his eyes open, his pupils fixed and dilated. His tattooed arms slumped by his sides, while Mimi screamed, wracked by bottomless pain. José Luis spoke to her and tried to help her up, but she didn't want to move. She couldn't. I leaned down in front of her and brushed her hair off her face. It took some time before she recognized me. "Teach?" She outlined a smile, bathed in tears. She looked around, and heaved a sigh. She kissed the corpse's still warm, moist lips, and closed his eyes with numb fingers. She frightened me with her irony: "A horse, Teach, a horse. My kingdom for a horse!" She curled up on the ground, as if trying to sleep. She put an arm over her dead boyfriend's chest and spread out Jacobo's flag like a blanket. "Until tomorrow, Fernando. Until tomorrow."

The last advance, the kids said, had been all-out carnage. There was no way to get through to the center. A furious army guy with a Cuban accent shouted through a loudspeaker that the Venezuelan people would never allow traitors to arrive at the Palacio de Miraflores, and that they would defend the Revolution to the last breath of their miserable lives. I jumped over the barricade and marched straight over the sandbags. I had to talk to them. I had to make them understand. As Moreira said, one of them must have retained a bit of softness in his sick heart. I knew if I conveyed my arguments with force, the confrontation would be resolved on good terms. I sidestepped the rubble, crossing the invisible line. I raised my arms and spread my fingers. A light breeze carried the smoke away from the road. I made out a line of soldiers standing a few meters away, with their rifles pointed at me. I took a few steps forward, but a brute force grabbed me by the shoulder, sharp nails digging into my forearm and forcing me to turn around. I saw Andrea's tear-stained face. Fear and distress prevented her from articulating any words. She managed to murmur: "No, Teach, no. Not you, please!" She was shaking and her teeth were chattering. "Don't go, Teach!" she kept repeating. I took her face in my hands and stroked her dirty hair. "It's okay, *mi niña*. Everything will be all right." "Nothing will be all right. Nothing is okay. Don't say it will be all right because nothing is all right." "You'll see. We'll soon be together at Giménez's bar." I kissed her forehead. I managed to pull away from her tight hug, from her furious heartbeat, from the forlorn lizard tattooed on her neck. The last thing I saw before I confronted the line of soldiers was her childish face, disfigured by anguish. I walked toward the enemy with my hands up. Silence invaded me. Everything seemed to be happening in slow motion. My plan was foolproof: I had to offer them sincere dialogue. I knew a deal was possible. Human reason and compassion would have to provide an irrefutable defense. After so much death, we had to sign a truce. "*Haja o que houver*" (Come What May) accompanied me as I walked toward them. Teresa Salgueiro's voice bolstered my resolve, gave me strength, and took me to unexplored places. Listening, I was led by memories and longing. I remembered Tatiana's birthday and the burned cake. We made love on the floor. We had been happy before the end of the world. When I opened my eyes, I saw before me a group of frightened children, disguised as soldiers, wearing uniforms that were too big for them. They were tired and scared. They didn't want to shoot. I could sense it. But their superiors harangued them and forced them to defend the dignity of the homeland. "They're kids, just kids! Can't you see that?" I screamed, convinced of the nobility of my cause. I was surprised by my own sense of confidence, my firmness, my belief in the mantra that we couldn't keep on annihilating ourselves because we were human beings. I imagined a speech I wasn't able to deliver. Everything I wanted to say was stuck in my throat, because they didn't let me raise my voice, because they weren't interested in hearing me, because the only thing they asked me to do was back away from the road. An angry and agitated officer struck the back of one of the kid-soldiers in the front row, barking out an order. Not all of them complied, but most were obedient. The first bullet tore my shoe open, hitting my big toe, but it didn't stop me moving forward. The second blast grazed my right ear, staining my temples with blood and making me lose my balance. Still, I stayed on my feet. I didn't stop walking, convinced I could fulfill my difficult mission. The third bullet knocked the wind out of me, striking me in the stomach and spinning me like a top. My feet slipped out from underneath me. I fell to the ground, fracturing my left leg. As I fell, I looked across to the mob. Mouths were agape and shock was etched on people's faces: "Teeeeeeach!" Consumed with fury, they rose up. José Luis, Esteban, Andrea, and Jean Carlo, holding rocks and broken bottles as weapons, flew over the sandbags. And behind them, enraged and unstoppable, ran the Azpurua brothers, along with Arias, Bastardo, Bejarano, Castro, Cifuentes, Córdova, Egan, Fernández, Granados, Heredia, López, Maita, Manrique, Méndez, Sánchez, Sandoval, Padrón, Pellico, Porras, Quirós, Torres, Valdés, Vera. Courage spread to the rest of the protestors, driving away their fear and exhaustion. Within seconds, the fierce stampede had crossed the street and swept past the barrier of soldiers. Bullets whizzed around them. Many fell, but others managed to cross the road. They fought in close combat with the scrawny soldiers. They grabbed the rifles out of their hands and beat them to death, splitting their skulls open. Two boys advanced on either side of Jean Carlo. They couldn't have been more than fifteen years old, one brown-haired and the other blond. They fell suddenly, struck down, with projectiles sticking out of their shaved heads. But Gordo remained in one piece, as if, for some unknowable reason, protected by fate. Strange hands grabbed me by the shoulders and dragged me to a clearing. I recognized the *Cascos Verdes* white helmets with the green crosses. It hurt to breathe. Countless people lost their lives that afternoon, but their fall did not discourage those who came up from behind. The advance was unstoppable. I don't know how long it lasted. I don't know if I stayed awake or asleep. The shooting suddenly ceased, giving way to the cries of the wounded and the wails of the survivors. On the ground, among the vanquished, I recognized the mane of brown hair, matted with fresh blood. The lizard on her neck was spattered with chunks of brain matter. What was left of Andrea had a broken bottle clenched in her fist, two holes in her temple, and a torn backpack with a book of poems by Mario Benedetti sticking out of it. The medics tried to lift me onto a motorcycle, but something stopped them. A strange, new sensation made our skin tingle, a déjà vu: the warmth of sunshine. After a year of darkness, the sky opened over Caracas and let in a tiny but precious beam of light. The sun, filtering through the smoke, traced a perfect rectangle of light onto Paseo Colón and a small part of the highway. The patch of golden sunlight was focused on a scene of pity: Mimi's kneeling figure, holding on to Román's body, placing his hand at the base of her belly, moving her lips, as if in prayer or making a solemn vow. Behind her, the light outlined the hexagonal contours of the Ríos Reyna concert hall in the Teresa Carreño Theater, one of the few buildings that had managed to remain intact.

A low-flying airplane broke the sound barrier. A pickup truck that had broken down on the bend opened its rear doors, brandishing a pair of giant speakers. The FM news broadcast interrupted the static. Elated journalists talked over one another, shouting and barely making themselves understood. Rebel forces had taken control of the military bases in Maracaibo, Valencia, and Maracay. In Caracas, the last line of military defense had been broken through by the crowd. The protesters had arrived at the palace. When the announcer, using a vast compendium of patriotic clichés, announced the longed-for freedom, people didn't know how to react. There was also despair among the jubilation. Little by little, the celebratory hugging began, mixed in with the nervous laughter and uncontrollable weeping of those who had lost everything apart from their lives, lives for which they had no more affection, lives in which they had no home to return to. José Luis and Esteban saw each other from a distance. They raced into each other's arms and kissed each other on the lips, grateful and in disbelief, patting each other, checking to make sure they were in one piece. Then they burst into tears. On the side of the road, with a wine-colored sweater wrapped around one hand and a bamboo steamer lid as a shield in the other, I made out Wong's silhouette. He was jumping up and down in a puddle and laughing like crazy. "We're *free*, brother, we're *free*!" he shouted. I also recognized my student, Marcel Hidalgo, aged and toothless, with a brass medal hanging around his neck. Gordo Jeanco was carrying him on his shoulders, a bloodstained flag with the stars torn fluttering behind him. The joy on Jean Carlo's face vanished when he looked around and couldn't find the person he was looking for. His expression changed completely. He sensed what had happened. The last thing I heard before I lost consciousness was the desperate cry of my little Orson Welles calling out for his best friend: "Andrea! Andrea! Where are you, Andrea?"

The *Cascos Verdes* asked me my name. I couldn't answer them. They put me on the motorbike again, but the street was impassable. When the motorbike jerked forward, I rolled onto the asphalt. And I never understood if the last images of my earthly life were real or just fragments of delirium, caused by my agony. I fell down without knowing if the sunlight was real or imagined. I fell down without knowing what would happen next, wondering if it had been worth all the blood that had been shed. "Give me time, give yourself time," whispered Tatiana from the mouth of a tunnel, standing in front of a birthday cake. And I collapsed without knowing if the kids, those who'd managed to save themselves, would end up leading decent lives or would become the same old villains, condemned by the ignorance of their forebears to perish in the ruins of their history. I collapsed without knowing if individual decisions can make a difference but with the certainty that the impulses of the human heart are the only defense we have against the unnerving sound of the trumpets of the apocalypse.

• • •

Tati blew out the candles. I kissed her invisible lips. The pain disappeared. Darkness. Peace. Silence. "I never realized how I lost you. Forgive me. *Haja o que houver,* come what may, I will always wait for you."

Author's Acknowledgments

From time to time, the aesthetic intentions of a writer connect with the social projects of people and institutions that are working tirelessly for the defense of human rights. The themes in *The Lisbon Syndrome* align closely with the work of organizations that seek to raise global awareness of the crisis in Venezuela that has been raging for more than two decades. One such organization is Saludos Connection, a nonprofit based in Texas that disseminates information about Venezuela's grave problems in both its health and education sectors to a world audience. It also advocates that change can be achieved through transformative cultural experiences. The publication of *The Lisbon Syndrome* enables us to continue and deepen our conversations about the power of literature to foster action and social activism, such as that undertaken by Saludos Connection.

I would like to thank Saludos Connection for its support, and I extend a special note of thanks to María Cristina Manrique de Henning and her family for their valued input with regard to the creative processes of *The Lisbon Syndrome*. Her belief in the power of writing as an agent of social change and of the responsibilities that writers have toward social issues and related problems was both inspirational and highly constructive for me.

Eduardo Sánchez Rugeles

Translator's Acknowledgments

Translation is a collaborative effort. I am grateful for the support and encouragement of Eduardo Sánchez Rugeles, Ruth Greenstein, Jeff Peer, Terry Deal, Isabel Moutinho, Christina Kramer, Josiah Blackmore, and Alicia Filev. Special thanks to my chess partner, Jim, for his endless inspiration and generosity.

Paul Filev